KAT'S SURRENDER

by

THERESA MARTIN GOLDING

BOYDS MILLS PRESS

Text copyright © 1999 by Theresa Martin Golding

Boyds Mills Press, Inc.
A Highlights Company
815 Church Street
Honesdale, Pennsylvania 18431
Printed in the United States of America

Publisher Cataloging-in-Publication Data
Golding, Theresa.
Kat's surrender / by Theresa Golding—1st ed.
[184]p. ; cm.
Summary: When Kat's best friend is hit by a car, she is torn between
loyalty to her friend and sympathy for the perpetrator, who suffers from
a mental illness.
ISBN 1-56397-755-9 Hardcover
ISBN 1-56397-074-0 Paperback
1. Friendship—Fiction—Juvenile literature. 2. Loyalty—Fiction—
Juvenile literature. [1. Friendship—Fiction. 2. Loyalty—Fiction.]
II. Title.
813.54 [F]—dc21 1999 AC CIP
Library of Congress Catalog Card Number 98-88232

First edition, 1999
First Boyds Mills Press paperback edition, 2002
The text of this book is set in Times Roman.

10 9 8 7 6 5 4 3 2 Hardcover
10 9 8 7 6 5 4 3 2 1 Paperback

To Jim and Cass for a great childhood,

to Jennifer, Michael, and Mary Kathryn,
that I may give them the same,

and to Gil, for everything

Chapter

1

KAT O'CONNOR WAS RUNNING late again. She stood in the corner of the gym, her green book bag slung over her shoulder, and watched the girls' basketball team practicing drills. Fran Riley whipped the ball at her. "Hey, Kat, take a shot."

"Can't, Fran. I gotta go." She had only stopped in to see how the team was making out so far this year without her.

"Come on, Kat." They were all standing watching her now. "Throw one up." Kat ran her fingers over the ball's bumpy surface.

"See if you've still got it, Kat," called Sue Clark.

Kat stood in place and dribbled. She still loved that feeling of the dropped ball returning to her waiting palm. But she didn't have it anymore. She didn't have that limb-stretching, heart-thumping feeling of exaltation that had made it so easy, that seemed to magically push the ball off her fingertips into its graceful arc to the basket.

Kat looked at the gym clock, caged in a metal box, then tossed the ball into the crowd of girls. "Sorry, but I'm real late." She turned and ran down the empty hall to the side door of the school. The sound of sneakers squeaking against the shiny court floor and the balls kissing the backboards and swishing down through the nets echoed after her. She didn't miss it all that much, really. Since her mother died she had too many other things to think about, and basketball was just a stupid game.

Kat slammed the bulky metal door behind her so hard that it bounced open again. She left it that way and bounded down the steps to the sidewalk.

"Kat!" Fran stood puffing in the open doorway. "Forgot your jacket. Catch!" Fran lobbed the rolled-up coat like one of her perfect half-court passes and it fell at Kat's feet.

"Thanks."

"Kat. Wait!" Fran hopped down the steps. "You sure you can't stay for practice?"

"Positive."

"But you can't just not play. We need you. St. Bernard's has a new center this year who's five ten. You know Allison won't be able to handle that."

"Give me a break," Kat said. "It's only Caitlin Rose. She grew three inches over the summer, but she still can't make a shot from anywhere outside the paint."

"C'mon, Kat. You have to play. I miss you. Why don't you just hang out at the practices and then decide?" Fran pushed her short brown hair back behind her ears. A smile spread across her freckled face. "Think about this. If you don't come to practice, when are we going to hold our Tyler Reid hate-club meetings?"

"Yeah," Kat sighed. "They were fun, weren't they? Remember the time I put the cockroach in his desk and it crawled right up his arm?"

"I never heard a boy scream like that," Fran laughed. "He hasn't even gotten you back for that one yet."

"He's such a creep." Kat fingered a spot on the back of her head where the hair was short and uneven. Tyler had spit a great wad of bubble gum there last spring and her mother had had to cut it out. It was disgusting.

Kat ran her hand over the sheared spot a few times, as her mother had once done with her long, cool fingers. "It'll grow in," her mother had said, her hands dropping softly to Kat's shoulders. "You won't even notice it before long." But the hole was still there, and she felt it every day.

The familiar lump began rising in her throat and Kat quickly turned away. She bent over her book bag and fiddled with the zippers, making sure each compartment was tightly closed. "I gotta go, Fran."

"But Kat . . ."

"I'll see ya." Kat swung her heavy book bag onto her back.

"Maybe we can go to the mall this weekend, just hang out or something, and we'll talk about it," Fran suggested.

"Maybe," Kat answered weakly, without turning around.

Kat shoved her hands into her pockets and started for home. It was a long walk. Back when she was training she used to run the whole way, books and all. There wasn't any reason to run anymore.

Kat looked up at the old maple trees growing by the curb. Their leaves were just starting to turn, the edges tipped lightly in gold and red. She felt so much like melting herself into the trunk of a big thick tree and stretching her arms up through the branches and her fingers up to the very edge of the twigs and being lulled by the breeze.

"Hey, Kat!" Helen Hogan, a short thin girl with a long blonde ponytail called down to Kat from her front patio. Helen lived on Cottman Avenue, across the street and just a half block up from their school, Saint Mary of the Assumption. Some of the kids called her "Helen the Hawk" because she flew out of class every afternoon and made right for her perch on that patio. She seemed to take particular pleasure in watching every kid pass by. She held vast amounts of information on who hung out together, which guys liked which girls, and which best friends weren't talking to each other. She probably kept better attendance records in her head than the nuns in the office did in their files. Kat figured that Helen would grow up to be one of those gossip columnists in the newspaper. Kat could just picture Helen at a Hollywood party, drinking in all the faces, the clothes, and the jewelry and scooping up every crumb of whispered conversation. Everything that went in Helen's ears came right out her mouth without any detours through her brain.

"Practice over already?" Helen asked, glancing up the street in search of other team members.

"I'm not playing this year," Kat said over her shoulder and kept walking.

Helen stood and gracefully glided down the steps to the pavement. "No kidding! Why not?" she called after Kat.

Kat turned and shrugged her shoulders. "I've got too many other things to do," she said sullenly. For someone so nosy, Helen didn't have a clue. None of them did. And if they were all so thick that they couldn't figure out the obvious, then she wasn't going to explain it to them.

When she had come back to school in September, Kat had wondered how she was going to deal with all the questions about her mother's death and how she was holding up under the strain and the sadness. She was worried about getting emotional and crying in front of the kids she hadn't seen all summer. But it never happened. No one even mentioned it.

Her house was on the northernmost boundary of the school parish. As she had walked home that first day with the crowd and watched them disappear one by one into their homes without even acknowledging her loss, she felt that they were all no different from the houses into which they had retreated: as silent and cold as the brick and as vacant as the picture windows reflecting the afternoon sun.

"They'll never win without you," Helen said and flitted back up the steps to her perch on the patio.

"Sure they will," Kat lied. The team probably wouldn't do well without her. She was the only one who had any height. At age thirteen she was already five foot eight and she had a deadly outside shot. She would root for them, of course, but she secretly hoped that they wouldn't make the play-offs. If they did, all her records from last year would seem like so much icing on the cake rather than the essential ingredient that helped the team rise to the top of its division.

Kat turned and headed for home again, keeping her eyes on the pavement in the hope that she could avoid meeting any other classmates. Kat's neighborhood in Northeast Philadelphia was a maze of blocks of brick and stone row houses. Large old trees thrived on the curbs between the cement of the sidewalks and the asphalt of the streets. Many houses had small, well-tended green lawns that sloped from the front patios down to the sidewalk below.

Kat turned the corner onto Rowland Avenue and waited at the light to cross over to Patton Circle. As the signal turned from red to green Kat watched the General. He was there on the circle every day without fail, mornings and afternoons, directing the hordes of pigeons that flocked around him to be fed.

"Company B! Flank right! Flank right!" The General flapped his arms, clenched his fists, and pulled air from the sky. His body moved in rhythm as though he were directing some large, reluctant marching band.

"Hi, General." Kat approached the front and waited for a break in the battle. The General leaned and swayed, barking orders and scattering bird food around the small, weedy traffic circle. Pigeons covered the ground and the wooden park bench, noisily pecking and cooing. They floated down from the rooftops of the surrounding blocks and they even sat on the General's shoulders and arms.

"Mr. Ellison! Pull back! Pull back!" The General, balanced on one leg, stretched his arms toward his favorite bird as it wandered too close to traffic.

Kat shooed Mr. Ellison back to the troops.

"Thank you, Kat, thank you." The General eased himself onto his wooden bench, his body stiffening after a day of battle and a lifetime of war. Above him, the real General Patton stood, uniformed, stoic, a proud look of determination frozen on his cast-iron face. Pigeons squatted on his head and shoulders, and his uniform was decorated with more than just medals.

"I brought something for the war effort, General." Kat pulled some bread crusts, saved from her lunch, out of her book bag.

"Do your duty then, girl." The General leaned back and stared absentmindedly across the battleground of his reign as Kat threw her few crusts to the birds, saving the largest piece for Mr. Ellison.

"Mission accomplished, sir!" Kat turned sharply and saluted, clicking together the heels of her regulation navy blue shoes.

"At ease. At ease."

"I brought something for you too, General." Kat rummaged in her book bag for a packaged cupcake. The General took it wearily, as though accepting his daily rations at the end of a long hard-fought battle.

"Ah, Kat, you're a good soldier."

"Can't I have a promotion then?" Kat stopped to see the General every day after school even though her friends all thought that he was really gross and her dad suggested that she avoid him. She had only spoken to him in the first place because she had lost a bet with Maggie, her best friend. And though she was frightened and mortified as she went into that first encounter, she found that she really liked the General. She went back to see him again and again until her visits became almost a daily routine. Maggie started refusing to walk home with her and Kat could see the stares and weird looks the other kids gave her as they passed by. But she didn't care.

She was like Alice in Wonderland, escaped through the looking glass into a new world. She conferred with the General on the proper deployment of troops, the problems of getting rations to the front, and the correct method of dealing with AWOL soldiers. She often wished that she could just curl up on the hard bench and let the afternoon fade away into darkness. Unlike Alice, Kat was in no rush to leave and would be perfectly content to be marooned on this island of nonsense.

Once the General had given her a little tarnished medal, hanging from a faded ribbon, and pinned it on the front of her uniform with great ceremony. He said it was an important honor and he even cried while he was bestowing it. She wore it to school the next day, but just for an hour or so. Even though she tried to explain its importance to everyone, it seemed that honors didn't transfer too easily between worlds. Her friends rolled their eyes and begged her to take it off. The boys started to call her Pigeon Lady and other, worse, names, and Sister Mildred was staring at her all through history class. Tyler Reid tortured her for a whole week over it, even pinning a bogus award to his shirt and strutting around the school yard mimicking her. So she just kept the medal at home in the small top dresser drawer where her hair ribbons were.

The General, for his part, never seemed to notice that that other world existed. Cars motored around the circle, always in a hurry, merging in and out and pushing out a noxious exhaust that, during rush hour, formed an unpleasant gray cloud above the circle. The surrounding blocks were full of houses with children who spilled out onto the sidewalks hiding, screaming, riding bicycles, darting between parked cars, or playing in the torrent of an open fire hydrant. Ambulances screamed up side streets to rescue heart attack victims or children who had swallowed a mouthful of laundry detergent. Men in trucks with big lifts came regularly to cut back and grind up with deafening noise the tree branches that dared to grow above the telephone and electrical wires. Ice cream trucks played their music, strollers rattled over the uneven pavement, parents hollered at their children and at each other, radios sang out from teenagers' bedrooms, and ball games cackled from living room televisions. It was endless and almost constant.

None of this existed for the General. He really never seemed to see it, never lifting his head to follow a passing siren or to search out the cause of a screaming child.

"But why can't I have one?" Kat knew that this wasn't real, but it did sometimes irk her that the General always refused to give her a promotion. It was like playing Gameboy but not being allowed to advance to the next level even though you avoided all the fireballs and you still had three lives left.

"Have what?" The General's attention span was sometimes very short.

"A promotion. I do deserve it, you know."

"But you're a woman, girl!" The General's response was always the same. No promotion was permitted. He was sorry about it but that was just the way it was. The game-board in the General's mind was a much earlier version than Kat's, and he had followed the old instructions for so long that his mind was locked into those rules and incapable of updating them.

"I even saved Mr. Ellison today. Why, if it weren't for me, he might be on the casualty list."

The General stiffened, his hands clenched tightly at his sides. "I know what you think. You think it was all my fault. It just flipped, I tell you. I tried to help him, I told you, I tried. . . ." The General's voice trailed off to a mumble. He was facing Kat but he spoke over her head. The General often spoke to people whom Kat couldn't see. This time, she knew, he was talking to the lady, Julia. The General spoke to Julia so often that Kat almost imagined that she, or the ghost of who she was, actually inhabited the little traffic island, floating around its circumference, passing through the iron Patton with the ease of transparency, and gliding carelessly to rest on the wooden bench.

The General fell silent but remained stiff, staring directly over Kat's head. Kat looked up at his tall, slightly bent frame. He didn't seem to wear his clothes so much as to let them hang there on him. He was like a large gangly scarecrow, untended and abandoned, a worn face poking out atop faded, soiled clothes and sagging straw. His fists were no longer clenched, but his hands, creased with age and browned by the sun, hung limply by his side. The muscles of his grizzled face twitched uncontrollably now as various emotions passed across it. To Kat it seemed as though the General were in a darkened movie theater watching a startling film. Only he had paid the admission price. He held the only ticket and she could only watch his face and guess at the scenes unfolding within.

She lifted the heavy book bag back onto her shoulders. "Good-bye, General," Kat whispered, as she slipped off his island and plunged into the world of noise and speed where she lived.

Chapter
2

"YOU FORGOT TO SPIT," Maggie called out.

The late afternoon sun warmed the pavement, feeding the budding grasses that had escaped the little patchwork lawns and put down roots in the parallel cracks in the cement. A pink lump of used bubble gum oozed toward shapelessness. Kat stepped over it. Maggie was sitting on her front steps twirling her long brown hair around her index finger.

Kat looked up. "What?"

"I said, you forgot to spit."

Kat climbed the seven steps to Maggie's front stoop and sat beside her. "I told you, Maggie, I can't spit anymore. If my dad catches me spitting again, I'll really be in for it."

"Well, fine, Kat. I don't care. But don't say I didn't warn you."

"Maggie, knock it off, will you?"

"Okay, okay."

Kat rested her head in her hands, closed her eyes, and let the sun soak into her face.

"Are you feeling okay?" Maggie asked.

"I guess," Kat answered slowly. "I'm just imagining. . . ."

"Well, you look like you're meditating. I read in this book once about these Buddhist monks in Tibet . . ."

"Maggie, I was just imagining that I was on a beach somewhere. I don't want to hear about Buddhist monks right now." Kat opened her eyes, her vision ruined. She stared at her nails, bitten low, the skin around them red and sore. "I just feel like getting away somewhere."

"Like where do you want to go?"

"I don't know. Away. A deserted island or something. The north pole. I don't care."

"In Tibet they have Buddhist monks and they're supposed to be good at helping people find inner peace. They'd probably be able to help you. You might have to shave your head, though."

Kat rolled her eyes. "I'm sure Tyler would volunteer to help me out with that one." She unconsciously ran her hand over the back of her head.

"Well, anyway, you can come in with me and hang out and watch television or something," Maggie offered.

"I can't. I gotta get Danny. I better go."

"Okay, but I think you should go back down to the pavement instead of cutting across the patios."

"You never give up, do you?"

"Nope. Just go down. I want you to see something."
Maggie was insistent.

Kat groaned, but she did get up. "This is stupid, you
know."

"Now look up," Maggie commanded.

"Up where?"

"You know." Maggie inclined her head to the right.

Kat froze. In the upstairs bedroom window of the end
house the curtains were held open, very slightly, and Kat
could just make out the dark outline of Twitch staring down
at her.

Mrs. Twitchell, or Twitch as the kids called her, was a
witch, and everyone knew it.

"Kat! Stop staring and get back up here!" Maggie
yelled, motioning to Kat with her arms. Kat jumped and
bolted up the steps, out of view.

"Why didn't you tell me she was there, Maggie?"

"I tried to warn you, Kat. I hate to tell you this, but I'm
pretty sure she cursed you." Maggie had this elaborate
theory that if you stepped on Twitch's property, you were
very susceptible to getting cursed. Twitch's powers were
much stronger there and the only way to counteract them
was to spit. All the neighborhood kids had been doing it
since they were very young.

"That's stupid," said Kat. "She didn't curse me." But a
funny tingling sensation began creeping up her spine and
tightening up around her neck like a long, thick, cold snake.
Just to be on the safe side, she walked across the concrete
patio and, looking furtively around, spit over the invisible
boundary line onto the witch's property.

"Too late," Maggie said. "You had to do it before you stepped off her property. If she cursed you, Kat, you're cursed."

Kat looked across to Twitch's property. The lawn was a tall mass of tangled weeds that spilled over onto the sidewalk and crept up from among the broken stones on her unkempt patio. Since Twitch's house was on the corner at the end of the row, she had a side yard, but it was hidden. A large untrimmed hedge rimmed the whole side of her property and obscured both her yard and a good part of the house. An evergreen tree of eight or nine feet, completely covered with a creeping honeysuckle vine, stood on a small plot to the rear of the house. The tree was being slowly strangled and it looked ghostly already, like a large hairy beast emerging from a muddy swamp, its arms partially raised, wrists limp. To Kat, the funny thing about it was that no matter how spooky it looked, there was almost nothing in the world that smelled so sweet as the honeysuckle in bloom in early June.

Kat looked up to find that Maggie was staring at her in a very funny way. Wisps of thin brown hair were wet against her small forehead and perspiration dotted her upper lip. "If you want to get uncursed, you have to swallow a goldfish." Maggie spoke solemnly.

"What?!" Kat cried. "A goldfish! Are you crazy or what? I'm not going to eat a goldfish. I never even heard of anybody eating a goldfish."

"People do," Maggie said. "I saw it on Nickelodeon just last week. I'll walk over to the Pet Emporium with you and get one. They don't even cost a dollar. We'll get a baby one and I'll help you swallow it. It'll be easy. You'll see. And you have to do it, really, for your own good. Something much, much worse could happen to you if you don't. If you wash it down with a Coke it won't even—"

"Forget it, Maggie," Kat interrupted. "I won't do it. It's too gross."

Kat stared at Maggie in disgust. Maggie's nickname was "the witch doctor" and she certainly looked the part right now. Her long brown hair was thin and wispy and so straight that not even the ends would turn up, but instead hung lifelessly around her shoulders and face. Her eyes were very large and of the palest blue, like two full moons set deeply in her small, thin, colorless face. Her nose was nothing but a small rise above the shapeless, pale-pink line of her mouth.

Maggie got her nickname because she was the expert in the neighborhood on witch's curses and cures. If you got sick with the flu or lost your lunch money, Maggie always claimed that it was because you had been cursed by Twitch. Then she would come up with some weird thing that you had to do to get rid of the curse. Kat knew that some kids rolled their eyes at Maggie's warnings and talk of curses, but even they half-listened to what she had to say. It was hard not to. Maggie constantly read books about the supernatural and knew almost every episode from the Ripley's Believe It or Not series. And no one could tell better stories than Maggie.

Poor Maggie lived right next door to Twitch and their houses shared a common wall. She always seemed to get cursed much more than any of the other kids. She even had this feeling that she was really a Russian princess descended from the last czar, and that Twitch had cursed her and brought her here to prevent her from ever assuming the throne. It was weird. She even said that she had recurring dreams of a time when she lived in St. Petersburg, with its spired buildings and softly falling snow. Kat didn't believe her, of course, but it was fun to listen to the stories.

And the whole thing was all the more strange in that none of the neighborhood kids, not even Maggie or Kat, had ever seen Twitch, even though she had lived in that broken-down house for as long as anyone could remember. No one ever saw her go out to the corner store for milk or down to the mall for clothes or shoes. She never took walks or sat out in the sun on a folding chair on a warm day.

They had been afraid of her and her ugly house ever since they were little kids. No one ever went to Twitch's door to sell Girl Scout cookies or wrapping paper. Sometimes you had to go onto her weedy lawn or patio to retrieve a ball, but you did it quickly and got right off. That's when you had to spit, to avoid a curse. Some kids were really worried about getting cursed, and some were doubtful but spit just to be on the safe side. Kat suspected that the older boys just enjoyed the spitting, shooting those loud, throat-clearing globs to impress their friends and gross out the girls.

They occasionally got lectures from their parents about how there were no such things as witches and that Mrs. Twitchell was just a poor, sick old lady. But Maggie was full of evidence to the contrary. She had books and magazines and an endless stream of stories about witchcraft. And it was creepy that Twitch was always peering out of her windows at them from behind her dark and always-drawn curtains. She had a fat gray cat that slinked around the neighborhood in all weather, and Maggie insisted that it was Twitch herself, transformed, scouting out her next victim or collecting the ingredients she needed for her latest curse. Sean Cassidy, who lived across the street, claimed to have seen her once, and he said she was the most hideous thing that he had ever set eyes on.

"All right, Kat, fine. But don't say I didn't warn you." Maggie shook her head.

"I'll take my chances, Maggie." Kat grabbed her book bag.

"I saw you with that old pigeon man again."

"So?"

"So, I'm telling you, one of these days, he's going to strangle you or throw you into traffic or something. Really, Kat, I know about these things."

"Well, I'm not worried."

"Well, you should be. There's something weird about him." Maggie twirled her hair around her finger.

Mrs. Darcy appeared at the side window and tapped on the glass, motioning for Maggie to come inside. Maggie turned her back to the tapping and stared straight ahead.

"I think your mom wants you," Kat said.

"Yeah, well, she can wait. Is she still looking at me?"

"No. She just left. Did you guys have a fight or something?" Kat asked, sitting back down beside Maggie.

"Yeah. It started when I was born. You just can't believe how much she gets on my nerves."

Kat bit her lower lip and looked up at the now-vacant window. "She doesn't seem that bad to me." Kat thought of all the small kindnesses Mrs. Darcy had done for her. The meals she had cooked, the wordless hugs—even her silent presence had been a comfort in those weeks after Kat's mother died.

"Oh, really? Well, then you can have her. You have no idea," Maggie sputtered. "You don't know how lucky you are to live with your dad. If I could live with my dad, my life would be totally perfect." Maggie kicked at the step below her feet.

Kat felt the blood rushing to her face. She hated how her body did this. Something little, something innocent, an old note fallen out of a book in her mother's handwriting, and it was like a little bomb going off inside her. Everything always had to rush upward, to her throat, and eyes and her face. Why couldn't pain travel downward to a less conspicuous place?

Maggie jumped up. "I'm sorry, Kat. I didn't mean that you . . . well, you know. You're not mad or anything, are you? I'm so stupid."

"No, it's okay." Kat stood and turned away, the ache dropping from her throat to the bottom of her stomach. "I gotta go."

"Do you think you can come out tonight?" Maggie asked. "We can have a wire-ball rematch—you, me, and Paul."

"Maybe," Kat answered slowly. "If I get my homework

done. My dad's been on my back since I flunked that math test last week."

"Yeah, I'm pretty disgusted too. You're not even worth cheating off of anymore. I liked it better when you were smart."

Kat walked away without answering. She had enough people on her case about her falling grades without having to listen to Maggie too. And what was it to them anyway? If she didn't care, what business was it of theirs? It was her life and she'd ruin it any way she wanted to.

Chapter

3

KAT LIVED ONLY THREE DOORS up from Maggie, and their houses, like everyone else's house on the block, were identical: same brick front, same concrete patio, same sloping green lawn. These houses were called straight-throughs because you could walk, with about fourteen straight steps, from the front picture window back through the living room, dining room, and into the kitchen where you could touch the back wall of the house. There were no corners to turn, no drawing room, family room or study, no sunporch or fancy deck.

Kat knew her house like a bird knows its nest. Each event in her life was laid there like a new twig, lining the walls and floorboards with strong memories that turned rather plain surroundings into a warm and comfortable home. She loved the mantel over the fake fireplace because it was there that she had displayed her school portraits and report cards and hung her Christmas stocking up with a small red tack pushed into the painted wood. She loved the little alcove in the dining room that her uncle had turned into a coat closet. She had hidden there often when she was little, playing hide-and-seek, feeling warm and special in the darkness, smelling the outdoor air that still clung to freshly hung coats, and feeling their cool softness as they hung about her head and brushed her cheek. She loved the greenish worn armchair in the living room where she seemed to fit just perfectly and so comfortably to watch television. She felt that she knew, as a friend, the low bookcase at the bottom of the stairs where she would often lie on her stomach and run her fingers across the covers of the books, drawing out with just a touch the memory of the characters and events in each one that she had read.

She stood by the bookcase and touched *The House at Pooh Corner*. She wished she were little again, in a world where bears could talk and endings were always happy.

"I'm home, Dad," Kat called up the stairs.

"You're late again, Kat." Kat's father appeared on the top step and frowned down at her. He was dressed in his usual button-down cotton shirt and wrinkled slacks. He rarely wore shoes in the house.

"I was right in the middle of an important phone call with Atlanta and I had to get off because I thought you weren't going to make it in time."

"Sorry, Dad. I just got caught up and . . ."

Mr. O'Connor sat on the top step and ran his fingers

through his hair. "It's all right, honey. Just get going, okay? You only have a couple of minutes to get there."

Kat's dad was a writer, but not the glamorous kind that Kat had once dreamed of becoming, having novels and poetry published in books with beautiful hardback covers. Mr. O'Connor was a technical writer. He took the garbled and halting language of specialists and translated it into English so it could be understood by the common person.

He used to have his own office before her mother died, but now he tried to do everything at home. It was nice to have him around in some ways, but she hated how they always had to tiptoe around the house and answer the phone in a certain way. And if you went into his room, you practically had to hold your breath so as not to disturb anything. When her mother was alive, she used to be able to go in there, still in her uniform, flop on the bed amid the fresh laundry, and tell her mother about the different things that had happened to her at school. Sometimes she would just lie there, lazily, breathing in the clean smell of the washed clothes and listening to the gentle rustling of the leaves in the tree outside the window, while her mother stood beside her and folded, putting everything in incredibly neat piles.

Kat let her book bag slowly slip off her shoulder and thud to the floor. She looked wistfully at the top shelf of the bookcase, where all her favorite books were lined up in a neat row. Beneath were those that she had wanted to read, classics her mother had helped her pick from the club selections offered at school every month. She hadn't read anything new in ages. Somehow she couldn't bear to go on alone into those cold unbroken pages. The new books stood like unfeeling strangers now and she ignored them, preferring to cling to the old friends on the shelf above. She pulled out *Anne of Green Gables*.

"Kathryn! Are you going or not?" her father said with mounting impatience.

"Okay. I'm going," she said sullenly.

"Look, Kat," Mr. O'Connor said, padding down the steps in his worn socks, "I'd go for him if I could, but I have to get back on that call to Atlanta. It's really important. You understand, don't you?"

"I guess," Kat sighed, her eyes filling up suddenly. She understood, but she didn't want to. She wanted her mind to be a blank, her heart unfeeling.

"Was there something you wanted to do?" her father asked, moving toward her. "If you have somewhere you want to go, I could run up and try to reschedule my phone conference. I could probably work it out." He put his arms out for just a moment, then jerked them up and ran his hands through his hair. These days, he often looked as though he were coming forward to hug her, but he always changed directions awkwardly at the last moment. He loved her. She knew that. She didn't need to be ritually kissed on the cheek every morning and evening. Displays of emotion had always embarrassed him. But she did wish that he would, maybe just one more time, hug her tightly like he had when she was a little girl. She remembered the feeling that time she had fallen at the playground and ripped a big gash in her head. He had kept his arms wrapped around her, even through the cleansing and the stitching, the wailing and the moaning. After it was all over, he had carried her to the car. She had put her arms around his neck and nestled her head against his chest.

"No," Kat answered. "It's okay. I'll get him." How could she tell him that what she most wanted to do was nothing, to crawl into a cave and hibernate, thoughtlessly, indefinitely.

"You better get going, then, or Danny'll be wandering off toward Torresdale Avenue and it will take us days to find him."

"Would that be so bad?" Kat asked half-jokingly.

Her father frowned. "Get going."

Kat put *Anne* down but tried to take the character's imagination with her. Maybe she could pretend that she was off to the orphanage to bring home a sweet-tempered and grateful waif. It didn't work. Danny was too annoying to be imagined away. He was his father's little "space cadet," never watching where he was going, never paying attention to what he should be doing. He crossed streets without looking, forgot his coat in freezing weather, and took reckless leaps from the top of the slide and the highest rung of the monkey bars. He lived in a world of cartoons and superheroes and dinosaurs, where everything was possible and only the bad guys got hurt.

After their mother died, Kat's father had had to switch Danny's kindergarten registration from St. Mary's to the Forrest Public School on Aldine Street. The public school had a full-day kindergarten program and her dad needed the time alone to get his work done. Since Kat's school let out first, she tried to help him by picking Danny up.

Kat hurried down the front steps. Even though she was late, maybe Paul would still be waiting to see her. She felt a little jump of expectation in her chest and quickened her pace up the street.

Chapter
4

"WATCH OUT!" PAUL YELLED. Kat had stepped in front of the number 99 school bus as it pulled up to take its place in line in front of the public school. The bus made a quick, squeaky stop as Kat slowly strolled over to Paul's front steps.

"Are you crazy?" Paul asked. "You walked right in front of that thing!"

"He saw me. He stopped," Kat said.

"Just barely. A few more inches and he would've hit you."

Kat shrugged. "No big deal."

She watched the idling school buses, lined up across the street from Paul's house. They filled the street with a low grumble and choked the air with diesel fumes. Paul knew that Kat picked up her little brother almost every day.

Though they never made any specific plans to meet, Paul was usually outside of his house at just the right time, bouncing a ball against his steps or fixing the chain on his bike down by the curb. Kat would hang out with him until the final bell rang and Danny's class was dismissed into the school yard.

Paul was in Kat's eighth grade class. They liked each other, but they had to keep it quiet. If word leaked out, they'd be tortured with taunts and rolled eyes and silly rhymes scrawled on the blackboard at recess. It was stupid to think that some kids still acted that way when they were all teenagers now. But that's what happened to Maggie and Jack Perkins, even though Maggie always swore that she hated his guts.

Kat waited at the end of her block each morning and Paul would come down the back driveway to meet her and they would walk to school together. They went up the back alleyways, avoided the main streets, and parted a block before the school yard. When the bell was rung and the kids filed in the side door, Paul would glance back and catch Kat's eye. They would say to each other with just a look, "We did it again." One of the things Kat liked so much about Paul was that they could talk to each other with just their eyes. His eyes were a deep brown, like melted chocolate, and she could look right down in them and know what he was feeling. It was like a special language only they could speak.

"I thought maybe you weren't coming today, Kat." Paul talked to the step below his feet.

"Well," Kat said, examining her fingernails, "I kind of got caught up talking to Maggie. It's a long story, but she says that she's sure Twitch cursed me today and that the only way for me to get uncursed is to swallow a goldfish."

"A goldfish!" Paul forgot himself and looked up at her.

"Yeah. Gross isn't it?"

A bell rang from somewhere inside the school.

"I guess I better go," Kat said.

Paul was staring up the street. A woman had gotten off the route 66 trackless trolley up at Frankford Avenue and was coming down the block. She had long dangling earrings and a whole head full of frizzy black hair. She carried a large cloth pocketbook that was stuffed to capacity.

"You better go," Paul said hurriedly, "or you'll miss Danny."

Kat backed up to make way for the woman to pass on the sidewalk. But she didn't pass. Paul was staring at the lawn and pulling up big clumps of grass.

"Hey, Pauly babe, your dad inside?" she asked.

Paul backed away from her up against the iron stair rail. "I guess," he mumbled.

"Thanks, hon." She patted him on the head, like he was a faithful puppy, and skipped up the steps into the house.

Kat could see the color rise from his neck and spread up across his face till even the scalp beneath his short, dark hair had turned red.

"I guess I better go," she said quietly to the ground.

Paul was rolling up a ball of plucked grass in his hand, squeezing it over and over, until the green stain worked its way out of the grass and onto his skin. He stood up on the top step and threw the damp wad as far as it would go. It sunk like a dying comet, shedding crumpled blades of grass as it flew.

"You coming out tonight?" Paul asked into his stained hands.

"Yeah," Kat answered. "Maggie wants to have a wire-ball rematch."

"What time?" Paul looked up.

Kat met his eyes and she could see that he wanted to come early, before Maggie, before the wire-ball game. "How about seven?"

"Sounds good." Paul smiled.

Kat smiled back, said good-bye without speaking, and hurried across the street to the school.

A flood of children came spilling out of the double doors into the blacktop school yard and rushed toward the waiting buses. Though Kat picked him up almost every day, Danny never looked for her when he came out the scuffed metal doors of his school. Most of the younger children would run to mothers who were waiting by the gate of the iron fence that rimmed the school yard and excitedly show off paintings and other artwork. But not Danny. He wandered around the school yard, rarely even toward the gate he had to exit, firing into the air at imaginary enemy aircraft or dodging in and out of other children as though pursued by invisible aliens. Kat always had to enter the school yard against the rush of children going in the opposite direction and pull Danny by the arm or shirtsleeve toward home.

"Come on, Danny," Kat said, grabbing his arm. "I want to get home quickly today. No fooling around."

In many ways, he was like an alien being to her. "What did you do in school today? Anything good?"

"I dunno," Danny said carelessly.

"What did you have for snack?"

"I can't remember. We had red juice, but mine spilled on Meghan."

"Danny! You have to be more careful. You have to learn to watch what you're doing," Kat lectured.

"It wasn't my fault," Danny shouted, stomping his foot and stopping just outside the fence. "Ryan bumped into me. Then Meghan kicked me and that's not fair."

"Okay, okay," Kat said. "Let's just get going."

Danny drifted along the sidewalk beside Kat, firing at passing cars, stomping on stray bugs, and whacking trees with a long stick that doubled as an imaginary rifle. Kat guided him around the corners, across the streets, and finally up the steps to home, where she deposited him in front of the television set.

For once, Kat plunged into her homework. There was a lot to do, and Paul was never late.

Chapter
5

AT SEVEN O'CLOCK Kat sat in the gathering darkness in the alleyway with her back against the cellar door. Every two houses on the block shared a small rectangular alley that led past the stone walls of their garages to the old wooden doors of the basements. The first and second floors of the houses rose up from over the garages and the basements so that in the alley the sky seemed small and far away and the shadows had a permanent home. It had been great for playing house and hide-and-seek in the old days when she and Paul and Maggie were little. Now it was a good private place to meet with no one to bother them but the ghosts of their former selves, pouring pretend tea, playing house and store, and lulling to sleep the plastic dolls in their cement beds.

Paul edged around the corner and stood with his hands in his pockets. "Hey, Kat."

"Hey, Paul."

"Want some gum?"

"Okay."

Paul flipped her a piece and she caught it in her right hand.

Kat popped the gum in her mouth and studied the wrapper in silence. Paul kicked a small stone back and forth between the walls. She knew he had something to say, but sometimes it took awhile for the thing to work its way out of him. He stood in the middle of the small alley and jumped straight up several times trying to slap the bottom of the cast-iron landing above them. The narrow landing, and the steps that descended from it into the driveway, provided a back exit from the house. Paul hit it on the third try.

"Do you remember the time when we were little and you almost fell off of there?" Paul asked with a grin.

"Yeah, I'll never forget," Kat laughed. "We were playing we were firefighters. I was supposed to be on the ledge rescuing a baby. As a matter of fact, I think that ledge part was your idea."

"No way," Paul said. "You were the one with all the crazy ideas. I can still see you hanging there, screaming. Your mom came flying out that door like..." Paul fell silent.

"Yeah, she did, didn't she?" Kat said quietly.

She was suddenly glad that so little light made its way into this alleyway and she leaned back into the corner of the cellar door. She looked up at the empty landing, remembering, feeling that frantic but sure grip on her wrists, being steadily pulled to safety.

Kat twirled the laces of her shoe around her finger. "Did you ever notice that nobody talks about their mom when I'm around? It's like it's embarrassing or something that I don't have one anymore."

Kat peeled the foil from the cellophane on the gum wrapper. "Like yesterday at lunch, Monica was going on about all this stuff she got at the Franklin Mills Mall, and when she gets to the part about what time her mom was picking her up, she looks at me, turns all red, and changes the subject."

"I don't do that."

"I don't mean you or Maggie. But everybody else does it." Kat rolled the gum wrapper up into a little ball. "It just makes me feel so . . . weird, like I have a strange disease that nobody can talk about in front of me."

Kat blew a small bubble with her gum, then cracked it between her teeth. "You gotta go to your mom's this weekend?"

"No. She's gonna be away at some conference in Atlantic City." Paul's parents were divorced and he spent every other weekend in New Jersey with his mom.

Paul picked up a stick, probably left in the alley from one of Danny's adventures, and began scraping at the mortar between the stones. He worked around a whole big block and then paused for just a moment. "Barbara's gone," he said quietly.

"No way!" Kat blurted. Paul's dad had had a succession of girlfriends since the divorce. Most of them had driven Paul crazy. But Barbara was cool. She even knew how he and Kat felt about each other.

"Yep. Gone. Just like that. You know that frizzy-headed lady you saw today? Well, welcome to life with Roseann."

"Oh, no," Kat groaned.

The kitchen door above them squeaked open and Danny crept out onto the landing. Paul moved back under the landing and out of sight.

"Danny, get back inside. You know you're not allowed out there," Kat said.

Danny stood up and leaned over the rail, searching for Paul. "Kat's in love. Kat's in love," he sang. "Kat and Paul, sittin' in a tree, k-i-s-s-i-n-g. . . ."

"Danny, if you don't get in the house, I'm going to tell Daddy and you'll be in big trouble. I mean no cartoons for a whole week." Kat threw her balled-up gum wrapper up at him.

Danny ran inside laughing and slammed the door.

"We better go," Kat said to Paul. "Maggie'll be looking for me soon. Meet you out front."

Paul went out the alley and up the driveway. Kat slipped in the cellar, went upstairs, through the house, and out the front door.

Chapter
6

KAT DIDN'T HAVE TO KNOCK for Maggie. She was already outside, bouncing a ball down by the curb. Paul was just turning the corner at the other end of the block and was heading down. It was still fairly light out. The sun sat for just a moment on top of the houses across the street, and the clouds in the west were colored like pools of melting orange sherbet. The small patch of sky above was warm and glowing and the air in the street below was turning crisp. Lights were blinking on up and down the row and the birds were making their last noisy flights before settling down for the night.

"Hey, Mags, ready to play?" Kat held out her hands and Maggie threw her the ball.

"Yeah. I'm dying to beat Paul twice in a row. Here he comes."

"Hey, Paul," Kat said as she bounced the ball against the curb.

"Hey, Kat." Paul looked up at the wires tinged in orange.

The wires for telephone and electric service were strung high above the street, stretched between wooden poles that were, to Kat's eye, but shorn and naked trees, stolen from the forests, stripped, sunk in concrete, and strapped with wires. She would sometimes pity them their fate. But not on wire-ball night.

Wire-ball was based on the game of baseball. Instead of a bat, the player had to throw the ball straight up into the sky and hit designated wires for a single, double, triple, or home run. If the opposing team caught the ball on the way down, it was an out. If no contact was made with any wire, it was a strike. Three strikes and you're out. Three outs and you lose your turn at bat, so to speak.

"How many innings do you guys want to play?" Maggie asked.

"Well, I gotta be in by nine, so let's play five," Paul answered.

"Afraid of getting beat again, Pauly?" Maggie taunted.

"Knock off the Pauly stuff, witch doctor. I let you win last week. I can beat you tonight with my hands tied behind my back."

"Yeah, right. We'll see."

"Can we just play?" Kat reached into her pocket. "I've got a quarter. Heads, Paul's up first. Tails, Maggie. I'll go last tonight. I don't care." Paul and Maggie's constant bickering drove Kat crazy and she sometimes withdrew from a game in disgust before it even began.

"Heads. You're up." Kat threw the ball to Paul.

The sun fell behind the houses and the streetlights on top of the telephone poles flickered on.

Paul stretched and smirked at Maggie.

His first throw hit the second wire up, a double, and bounced off at an odd angle just out of Maggie's reach.

"Good one, Maggie," Paul sneered as he came forward for his next throw.

"Just shut up and throw," Maggie retorted.

Paul leaned back and threw with all his might. He missed every single wire and the ball came back down with a loud thwong right on the hood of Mr. Hooperman's new Jeep Cherokee.

All three kids scattered and ducked behind other cars parked up the street. But Mr. Hooperman never appeared, and they casually went back to the game as if nothing had happened.

"Great one, Paul," Maggie whispered out of the side of her mouth. "Why don't you just put the next one through Hooperman's living-room window?"

"Why don't I just put the next one right through your mouth?" Paul responded.

"Come on, you guys, knock it off, will you?" Kat spoke to them both, but she caught Paul's eye long enough to let him know that she was blaming Maggie and not him. He knew, and smiled back.

Paul's next throw would have been a single, but Kat

caught it on the way down. One out. On his next shot, he doubled and drove in one run.

"All right! All right!" In the absence of a teammate, Paul high-fived the telephone pole, a ritual boys seemed obligated to perform every time they scored a run. Kat and Maggie rolled their eyes.

Paul was still up with one run in and a man on second. Only one out.

"One, zip," he called out as he wound up. "You guys better get ready because here comes a two-run homer."

Maggie and Kat stood, bodies tensed, arms bent, ready to dart in any direction the ball might fly.

Paul let go of the ball and he was right, he had called it. It hit the home-run wire, got tangled up in the triples wire, and flew out over Kat's head toward the "outfield" which was covered by Maggie. She would really have to run to get it, and she was determined. Kat and Paul stood, frozen, and watched her, eyes squinting to follow the dark ball against an ever-darkening sky. She drifted backward now, arms outstretched, the ball falling right toward her waiting hands. At just that moment, a large gray car with one headlight spun around the corner and hit Maggie square in the back. There was a sickening crack, and then a dull thud as she was flipped up onto the hood, then thrown to the side, landing on the hard asphalt. The ball rolled down the street just out of reach of her now motionless hand.

Chapter
7

"MAGGIE!" KAT SCREAMED and ran to her friend. "Help! Help! Somebody come!"

Mr. Hooperman ran down from his front porch, jumping all seven steps in one leap.

"The license, the license number. Somebody get the license number," someone called out.

Paul raced up the street after the speeding car, his sneakers slapping against the black asphalt.

The whole street was coming alive. A siren sounded in the distance, neighbors up the street stood on their front porches, smoking cigarettes and leaning over their rails, while neighbors from down the street, Maggie's neighbors, came down to the sidewalk with concerned faces, leaving dinners, dirty dishes, and the evening news behind. Children came from everywhere, from blocks around, pushing, shoving, climbing on cars and shimmying up poles, wrestling with each other for better position to see the unconscious girl in the street.

Maggie was absolutely still, her eyes closed. Kat hovered over her, helplessly, like a mother bird whose baby has fallen from its nest. She crouched beside her. "Maggie! Maggie, can you hear me?" she whispered, just above her friend's head. "Oh, Maggie, please, please be all right."

Mrs. Darcy flew into the street and dropped to her knees beside her only child. She began stroking Maggie's arm and mumbling, with eyes closed, as if in fervent prayer.

The ambulance arrived and the paramedics pushed Kat back out of the way. They were bundling Maggie up, taking her away. The police were moving people back, asking questions. Kat hadn't noticed, but her father was there, his arm around her shoulder. He began slowly moving her toward home. For the second time that day, she had that cold, snakelike sensation, but this time, it was inside her, coiling around her stomach and ribs and making it hard to breathe.

Remembering, she looked up and saw the black outline of Twitch in the second-floor window, hovering over the whole scene like the ringmaster of the wretched circus below her.

"Excuse me. Just a minute there." A large, heavyset policeman was pointing toward Kat and trying to extricate himself from the milling crowd. "Are you Kathryn O'Connor?"

"Yes, she is," Mr. O'Connor answered. "And I'm her father."

The officer puffed his way over to them. With every movement that he made, a fat wad of keys jangled against the nightstick hanging from his belt. "I'm Officer Morales," he said, patting the name tag on his chest. "One of the neighbors back there said that your little girl may have seen the accident. Did you see it, Kathryn?"

Kat nodded at the big man. His blue uniform was wrinkled and stained under the arms and he smelled of onions and pickles, as though he had been in the middle of a McDonald's hamburger when the call about Maggie came over the radio.

"Okay, honey. Why don't you tell me just what you saw." The policeman pulled a small notebook and pencil from his back pocket and looked at Kat. "Whoa! Wait a minute. Wait a minute. I think you better sit down."

Kat had been leaning against her father and was surprised to find that she was trembling. As her father helped her toward the steps, her legs wobbled beneath her and she felt as though her bones had somehow turned to Slinkys. She took a seat on the top step.

"You okay now? This won't take long. You just relax." Officer Morales patted her knee awkwardly and squatted down in front of the steps. "Now why don't you go ahead and tell me what you saw."

"I don't know," Kat mumbled. "It happened so fast. Maggie was running back, trying to catch the ball, and then this car just came spinning around the corner and hit her."

"Can you describe the car for me? Do you know what color it was? What model?"

Kat hesitated. "Well, I guess I didn't pay much attention. Like I said, it happened so fast. It didn't seem to have a color. It was sort of gray, I guess."

"Do you know the make of it? Was it a Toyota or a Chevrolet? Was it a new or an old car?"

"It wasn't new," Kat said. "It was kind of a big, old car. I don't know what kind it was or anything."

"Can you describe the driver? Was it a man or a woman?"

"I don't know. I don't know," Kat said anxiously, biting on her thumbnail. "It happened so fast. I was over there, across the street. It was dark out. At the last minute I saw this headlight coming. I didn't even have a chance to warn her. And then Maggie was thrown up in the air and I ran to her. I should've watched the car, shouldn't I? I should have gotten the license. I just didn't think. I just ran to Maggie. I'm sorry, I . . ."

"It's okay. It's okay," the officer reassured her. "You did just fine. You did the right thing going to your friend. That was the most important thing." Officer Morales stood with a grimace and rubbed his hand across the small of his back. "Don't worry," he said, nodding to Mr. O'Connor. "We've got a portion of the license number. We'll get this guy." He gave Kat a pat on the shoulder and walked stiffly back to his patrol car, the keys jangling against the swaying nightstick.

Kat looked up at her father. "I could have gotten the license number if I looked. I just didn't think. It's just that Maggie was lying there . . ."

Mr. O'Connor put his index finger on her lips. "It's okay," he said quietly. "It's all over. Don't think about it anymore." And he put his arm around her and helped her into the house.

Chapter
8

When Kat came down for breakfast the next morning her father was at the kitchen table with the morning paper and a cup of coffee. His dark wavy hair was uncombed and the gray strands that started appearing last year coiled out from his head like the springs of a broken clock. He wore glasses on the end of his nose when he read, and he didn't see Kat come in. She slipped into the seat across from him.

"Is it about Maggie?"

"What? What I'm reading here, you mean?"

"Yeah. Can I see?" Kat leaned across the table, hungry for the news.

"There's not much here. It just describes the accident and gives a description of the car. They have some bits of the license number."

"I bet Paul's the one who got the license."

"Maybe." Mr. O'Connor pulled the paper toward himself and turned the page to the sports section.

"But how's Maggie, doesn't it say? Did you talk to Mrs. Darcy?" Kat's stomach was rolling and she clenched her hands together on her lap.

"Kat, I'm sure she'll be okay eventually, but it might take a little while," her father said softly. "I'll call Mrs. Darcy today and I'll fill you in on everything when you get home, okay? Now don't worry." He got up, came around the table, and did that funny thing with his arms again. He leaned toward her and she thought for a moment that he was going to hug her, but he changed directions at the last moment and reached for the sugar bowl instead. He stood behind her and patted her on the back. "Look at the time. You didn't even eat or pack your lunch yet. You'll be late again."

"We don't have any bread. I was going to go to the store right after the wire-ball game, but . . ." It was Kat's job to keep the house stocked with the essentials from the corner store. Her dad did the weekly shopping at the supermarket.

"It's okay. My wallet's on the mantel. Just buy a sandwich at Tony's on your way to school and I'll pick up bread when I take Danny in."

"Thanks, Dad." Kat threw on her coat and grabbed her book bag. Her stomach was too upset for breakfast.

"Dad?" She lingered in the doorway and held her breath. She couldn't seem to ask him.

He was stirring his coffee round and round. He looked

up at her over his glasses. His eyes were a soft gray, like a kitten's fur, and they seemed to be always inviting you to trust and to relax. "Kat, honey, she's not going to die," he said quietly.

"You're sure?"

"I'm sure. The paper says that she's in stable condition."

Kat let out her breath in a great sigh of relief, and ran to the front door with a lighter step. Danny was just coming down the steps rubbing his eyes. "See ya, Danny Boy."

"I'm not Danny Boy!" he whined. "Don't call me that!"

"Okay, okay, cranky."

Danny stuck his tongue out at her.

Kat shook her head and hurried out the door.

The morning was crisp, but clear, with the promise of warmth by afternoon. The lawns and bushes were wet with dew and you could just see your breath. Kat waited for Paul on their corner, just beyond Twitch's wild hedge.

She closed her eyes for just a few moments and tried to recall her dream from last night. She had dreamed about her mother every night now for over three months, ever since she had died. Sometimes, she remembered it as soon as she woke up, but other times the memory of the dream would come flooding over her suddenly while she sat in class or was out at recess and she would have to deal with the sadness in front of all those people who didn't understand. She tried to think of it now so that she could get it over with here, alone. It's not that they were always bad dreams. Some were good, but even then, they reminded her of all that she missed. A lot of the times, she dreamed of the last time she had seen her mother.

Chapter
9

IT WAS A SUMMER NIGHT and the windows were open. She was aware of the commotion first before she heard the far-off wail of the ambulance and she knew that they were coming to her house. It had happened three times before. She lay in bed without moving and watched the faint rustling of her bedroom curtain. A large knot was forming in her throat and she began to say the Hail Mary silently over and over again until it was merely a meaningless chant, a musical blur of words. She listened to the banging of the front door, the heavy stamping of feet up the stairs, the short, brusque commands of the medical people to each other and the clanging of the metal sides of the stretcher.

When she heard them going down the steps, she rose and with sweaty hands quietly opened her bedroom door. It was such a small house. They were having some trouble maneuvering the stretcher between the wrought-iron stair rail and the wall. Her mother's eyes were open and her head swayed side to side as they jiggled the stretcher down. She wished that she hadn't looked, afterward, because she could never forget those eyes. Her mother was there, seeing and knowing, feeling and understanding, but she was trapped inside a sick and useless body and she couldn't get out. She was kind of like the Tin Man in *The Wizard of Oz* before Dorothy had found him. She was in there, but her body was rusted and useless and there were no oilcans in sight.

Danny didn't stir. He hadn't any of the other times either, but she went in to check on him after they were gone. He was sleeping soundly, blissfully ignorant, surrounded by the plastic dinosaurs he had taken to bed. She pulled the sheet up over his shoulders and looked out his window into the back driveway. All the houses were dark and quiet. Everyone slept on, undisturbed, as though nothing had happened, as though it didn't matter.

Kat had walked silently in bare feet back to her bedroom. She could hear the faint clink of rosary beads and she knew that Mrs. Olshefski, their next-door neighbor, was downstairs, as arranged, to care for her and Danny in their father's absence.

She had lain back in bed and watched the swaying cobwebs that hung from the corners of her room and wondered how they formed, how all those seemingly invisible pieces of dust managed to meet at the same place, attract and stick together in a chain. "Oh, my Lord!" her mother would have said had she seen them, and she would have swiped at them with whatever was handy, an old towel or pair of slacks draped over the bed, bound for the hamper, and they would have disappeared, the hundred little particles scattered into nothingness again.

The cobwebs had had full reign and the whole house was in disarray since her mother had gotten sick with the cancer in late March. Her parents had tried to prepare her, to gently explain what would ultimately come to pass, but she didn't want to hear it. She knew anyway, and it didn't make her feel better to have them actually say it out loud. She preferred to be numb about it and to just glide gently through the days. It was like floating on a river in a flimsy raft. She knew the waterfall was ahead, but she preferred not to dwell on the inevitable plunge, but only to feel the sway of the rippling water and to watch the passing trees and the clouding sky.

She had spent the long hot days of June in the front bedroom with her mother with the window air conditioner humming and drowning out all sounds of the outside world. They would read and talk. Kat liked to bring her mother lunch and dinner and all the news from the block. Sometimes, they just sat quietly and listened to the rumble of an approaching thunderstorm or their own thoughts. Her dad could never understand how they could do that, when he would find them that way, just sitting doing nothing. But Kat and her mother had always enjoyed each other so much, and there was something very peaceful about just being together, lying on the bed staring at the ceiling, each traveling around in her own thoughts, but safe in the company of the other's presence.

When her father had come home early the next morning, she knew that it had happened. She had dozed off, but she heard the front door open and the muffled exclamations of sorrow of Mrs. Olshefski. He came up the stairs slowly and she was already crying before he came into her room. "Kat," he had said, "it was for the best. She's not suffering anymore, honey. I know that she . . ." But Kat was sobbing and he couldn't go on. He patted her shoulder. "If you need me . . ." His voice choked off and he had to leave the room. She had turned toward the wall and cried in great painful sobs.

It was just so hard for her to believe, even now, that her mother was gone. She still felt her so much. It was like they were in the same house, but in different rooms. There was just a wall between them, but they couldn't get through to each other and all she could do was stand on her side frustrated and alone.

Chapter
10

KAT SHIVERED AND LEANED to zip up her coat. Paul appeared in the distance. She quickly turned away, toward the breeze, and wiped her sleeve across her face. He was rushing down the street, his green book bag slapping against his leg, his rumpled blue jacket open and flapping in time with his gait. His face was tightly screwed up and his mouth hung half open as if he expected to catch the news about Maggie like a fish catches a sinking morsel of food.

His chin dropped, he slowed down, and he approached Kat reluctantly when he saw her face.

"It's bad, isn't it?" he said.

Kat smiled. "No, no. It's okay," she sniffed. "Well, actually, I don't know all of what's the matter, but I know that she isn't going to die or anything really bad like that." She told Paul what her father had said and Paul told her of the chase after the car, the posses that the kids formed to track it down, the searches they made up and down the dark alleyways for clues until it got late and they had to go in.

"Were you the one who got the license number?" Kat asked.

"Yeah. But I couldn't get it all. If I had just been a little faster, I might have seen it. It's weird, but I just froze when it happened. If only I had turned right away . . ."

"They should have put your name in the paper," Kat interrupted. "If it weren't for you, they probably wouldn't even have a chance of catching this guy."

Paul smiled and looked down at his shoes.

Today, their walk seemed much too short and they were at the school yard before they knew it. But there was no need to separate. Just about everyone in the school yard had heard about Maggie's accident and they were just waiting for Kat and Paul to fill them in on all the details. Now that she knew that Maggie was going to be okay, Kat was enjoying the event of the accident. She didn't really mean to, and she did have some momentary twinges of guilt, but they were like small stones in a rising river, surrounded and then submerged by the gush of excitement and the flood of attention that she was now receiving. Not only did her classmates surround her, but she felt the interested stares of the other kids too. She squared her shoulders and smoothed her plaid uniform. She was conscious of the way her dark hair, drawn back in a ponytail and naturally curled at the end, flipped from side to side as she turned her head, adding emphasis to everything she said.

Chapter
11

S⊤. Mᴀʀʏ's ᴡᴀs ᴀ ɢʀᴇᴀᴛ stone edifice that, together with the parish rectory and convent, took up a full city block. It seemed to Kat like a medieval castle with its thick high walls and stone archways that led to inner courtyards. Four city streets formed a square moat around its perimeter and separated it from fields of brick row houses that stretched out for miles in every direction. St. Mary of the Assumption was its patron saint and stood out front on a green lawn beneath two bowing trees. Sculpted in white marble, the Blessed Mother's veil and ankle-length cloak covered all but her serene face, her perfect toes, and her outstretched hands.

Fran Riley came rushing through the arch into the school yard, her blue knee-highs collapsed around her ankles, and burst into the circle where Kat was talking. "Oh, my gosh, Kat! I can't believe you're here! What happened to Maggie? Are you okay? I just heard on the way to school. What happened last night?"

"Maggie's in the hospital, Fran. But she's going to be okay," Kat said, biting on her lower lip and feeling an unexpected catch in her throat.

"But what about you?" Fran asked, dropping her backpack and pulling up her socks. "I was such a wreck. I ran almost all the way. Then Tyler told me that you got hit too and the doctors weren't sure whether you were going to make it."

Kat's mouth dropped, but she kept her eyes on Fran. Tyler was such a gutless coward. He wasn't happy unless he was playing cruel jokes, bullying little kids, or shooting squirrels with his BB gun. Kat wouldn't give him the satisfaction of showing her anger. She was sure that he and his goony friends were lurking nearby, just waiting to see her reaction to his lies.

"In his dreams," Kat said to Fran. "Don't ever believe anything that creep says. I'll tell you exactly what happened." More kids were coming into the school yard and they all quickly joined the crowd standing close around Kat and Paul. Kat began her story again, giving every detail of the accident, and Paul followed up with a report on the efforts of some of the kids to track the mysterious gray car. Helen Hogan elbowed her way into the middle of the throng and hung on every word that was said.

Before they could quite finish their story, the bell rang. At the sound, the kids fell mostly silent, as required, and separated into their classes, each to the spot on the asphalt reserved for their homeroom. In two single-file lines they entered the building with little sound but the tap-slide tap-slide of navy blue shoes and loafers on the slate steps.

As the class headed up the steps to the second floor, someone on the landing above dropped his math text. It fell like a missile, grazing Kat's head and crashing with a thud at her feet. Kat jumped backward, almost losing her balance.

"I'm soooo sorry," Tyler said with a smirk as he sauntered down to where Kat was standing. "That book just slipped right out of my hand."

Kat put her foot on the math text just as Tyler bent to reach for it. "Here, Tyler, let me get it for you," Kat said sweetly. She picked up the book and dangled it in front of his face. Before he could grab it, she flung it to the bottom of the steps. "Oh my, Tyler. You were right. That is a slippery book." Kat leaned toward Tyler and lowered her voice. "Next time I have to touch it, it might just slip out the window."

"Ooooh," Tyler retorted. "Threats from the pigeon girl. I'm so scared."

Kat ignored him and went up the steps to her classroom. Kat, Paul, and Maggie were all in the same homeroom, which was good, except that they had Sister Mildred. There were five nuns left teaching at the school, and two of them, Sister Dolores and Sister Mildred, were to be avoided at all costs. Last year, Maggie had had Sister Dolores. It was just Maggie's kind of luck to always get the worst room assignments. Paul had Sister John. She could be a little boring, but she was very sweet.

Kat was the one who had all the luck in seventh grade. Kat had Mrs. Bennett. Not only was she a great teacher—they went on fossil hunts, raised chicks in the classroom, and solved mysteries with math problems—but she was kind and calm and always seemed able to sense when things weren't going too well at home for Kat. She overlooked Kat's late homework and missed assignments. Mrs. Bennett even came to the viewing, concern etched in the lines around her eyes and in the set of her jaw. While most of the mourners lingered with and comforted her dad, Mrs. Bennett had come for Kat. "Write about it," she had whispered to Kat just before she left. "It will help."

All year Mrs. Bennett had told Kat that she was a gifted writer, praising her compositions, marveling at the beauty of her words. And it did help when her mother was sick, to gather up all the fractured pieces of her thoughts and feelings and pull them together in her journal. But after her mother died, the words inside all went cold and whatever she tried to write came out flat. Mrs. Bennett still stopped her in the hallways sometimes and asked how the writing was coming. "Just fine," Kat always lied. She didn't know where this power to write came from in the first place. And now that it was gone, she certainly couldn't explain where it went.

The change from Mrs. Bennett to Sister Mildred was drastic. Sister Mildred made their lives miserable. And it wasn't just because of her nasty temper. Sister Mildred made fairly regular trips to the neighborhood to visit some of the old people on their street, even Twitch. Paul thought that the visits were part of the parish outreach program for senior citizens. Maggie was convinced that it was something more sinister, that Sister Mildred was the convent spy, out to gather dirt on all the kids.

It was annoying. Kat and Maggie would be hanging out or goofing off in their own back driveway and they'd look up and see her standing motionless at the end of the block watching them. She had even given them detention for draping toilet paper in Mr. Hooperman's tree one Saturday night. They never could figure out how she knew they did it, since even their parents didn't know.

On the last day of seventh grade, they found out their room assignments for the next year. It ruined what should have been a sweet day of celebration, and made them savor each passing week of summer as their last delicious taste of freedom before a long, dreary school year.

Maggie blamed it all on Twitch. The week before on trash day, there had been a wild storm with high winds. The Darcys' can blew over and the trash spilled onto Twitch's property down by the curb. Mrs. Darcy made Maggie clean it up and, even though Maggie spit profusely while doing it, she said she felt like one of those ducks at the firing range, an open target with nothing to hide behind. She just knew some sort of curse was coming.

"Are you going to tell Sister Mildred about Maggie?" Paul asked as the kids fumbled in the crowded coat room putting away their things.

"I don't know," Kat answered. "I guess. If she asks, I will. The story was in the newspaper, so she might know already anyway. Why don't you tell her?"

"Why should I do it?" Paul asked.

"Because I didn't do that math homework and I'd just rather that she didn't notice me."

Paul gave her a half smile as they headed out toward their desks and she knew that he would help her out.

Sister Mildred lumbered into the room. She was an older nun, large and rather heavy. The kids had nicknamed her Turtle, both because of the slow and ponderous way in which she moved and her tendency to snap at anyone who got in her way. Her habit, like that worn by all the nuns in her community, the Sisters of the Immaculate Heart of Mary, was long sleeved and fell below her knee, and the blue veil and starched white coif that seemed to pinch into her temples never allowed even a single strand of hair to stray into public. Once she made it to her desk in the mornings, she settled in and didn't move except in cases of emergency. But whatever advantages she had lost with her lack of mobility were more than amply compensated for in the quickness of her eyes and her sharp commanding voice.

"Stand for prayers." She ordered the children and they obeyed with the short morning recital asking for blessings upon their work.

"Take your seats. Mr. Powell, where is your tie?"

"Sister, I—" Jason Powell attempted to respond.

"Stand, sir, when you speak."

"I, I forgot to remember it," he stumbled.

"You forgot to remember it? How interesting. You will immediately put your name on the board in the probation column. And if you forget to remember tomorrow, you will move your name to the detention column. Perhaps that will help your memory."

Jason did as he was required, squeaking out his name with yellow chalk on the growing list and returning to his seat with a smirk and rolling eyes to let all the boys know that he was not the least bit concerned.

"Pass all homework forward. Anyone whose homework is not complete will stand in the back of the room."

No one rose.

"Very good. Open your math texts to page 23. Emily Peters, Matthew DiRienzo, and Carolyn McFadden to the board please. Let's see problems two, four, and six."

Kat breathed a sigh of relief and crouched down in her seat. The unlucky students rifled through their books to the correct page and swallowed excessively on their way up to the blackboard. They were slowly screeching out the numbers with their chalk when there was a knock at the front door of the classroom. Mary Kathryn Monahan, who sat in the first seat of the first row, jumped to answer the door and quickly returned to whisper something in the Turtle's ear. She actually rose, with as much speed as she was capable, and hobbled to the door, pausing only to warn the class not to utter a word in her absence.

"Yo, DiRienzo," hissed Jimmy O'Reilly. "You're way off. You gotta get the x on the other side of the equation."

DiRienzo issued a childish curse and praised God for that timely knock on the door all in the same breath. He dashed down the aisle, absorbed the figures in Jimmy's copybook, and returned to confidently and quickly complete the problem on the board.

Kat was stretching her neck in vain to see who had

interrupted the class when Paul, who sat nearer the front, turned and caught her eye. When she saw the look on his face, she knew in an instant who it was. Kat mouthed the words "Mrs. Darcy" and Paul nodded stiffly. The door reopened and Sister Mildred called out, "Kathryn O'Connor, please come here."

Kat rose, glancing at Paul's white face.

"Shut the door behind you, dear," Sister said. She turned toward Kat. "You are to go to the hospital with Mrs. Darcy. Your father knows that you are going and has given his approval. You will be excused from school for the rest of the day. Mrs. Darcy will see to it that you get home."

Kat looked at the two anxious adult faces staring at her. She swallowed twice. "Did something happen to Maggie?" Perhaps her father had been wrong. Kat's heart was beating rapidly. Like the rubber ball they had played with last night, it seemed to be bouncing frenetically, front to back, front to back between her chest and back.

"No, no. It's okay, Kat. There's nothing for you to worry about," answered Mrs. Darcy.

Sister Mildred rested her arm on Kat's shoulder and was unconsciously stroking it as she discussed with Mrs. Darcy a plan for Maggie to make up her schoolwork. She had that faint perfumed smell about her that all the nuns seemed to share. Kat wondered whether it was a special convent soap or a laundry detergent manufactured by the Vatican and sent to all the convents around the globe. It was the smell of the back corners of neat bureau drawers, of dark, little-used rooms in large houses, and of the empty and dimly lit church early in the morning before mass has begun.

"Are you ready, Kat?" Mrs. Darcy was speaking to her.

"I guess . . . but I think maybe . . . should I get my books?" Kat stammered.

"That's all right, Kat. You will be excused from homework tonight." Sister Mildred removed her hand from Kat and turned her over to Mrs. Darcy for the day. She turned in her slow, ponderous way back into the classroom, and the closed door muffled only slightly the sharp commands that she was issuing to regain control of the restless class.

Chapter
12

MRS. DARCY'S CAR was an old, dark green Chevy Nova that Maggie affectionately called "the Tank." The passenger side door was dented in so much that it couldn't be opened and Kat had to crawl across the driver's seat to get in. There were so many holes covered with colored masking tape in the vinyl seats that Kat felt as though she were sitting on the skin of a diseased leopard. The outside of the car was pockmarked with quarter-sized rust stains where the paint had peeled away so that, as Maggie often said, the Tank looked as though it had come under artillery fire in some recent war.

Mrs. Darcy drove in silence and Kat alternately watched her and the midmorning traffic while she picked at the peeling tape that was scratching and sticking to her legs.

Normally Kat was uncomfortable when she was alone

with such an adult. The mothers and fathers of her friends would always try to make interesting conversation, asking her the same old questions about school and classes and making the same tired jokes about boyfriends. It was like the constant drip, drip of the bathroom faucet. It was slightly annoying but it filled the silence and you even got used to its rhythms. But when it stopped, when parents ran out of their stock questions, you would begin to notice how warm and uncomfortably still it was. Kat would sit awkwardly then, looking at those blank, smiling adult faces. She would drop her eyes to the floor and rummage in her mind for the right tool to turn the conversation back on, to resume the drip, drip that fills up the silence of the night.

But with Mrs. Darcy, Kat could relax. Mrs. Darcy didn't make small talk. She rarely spoke at all. And since conversation wasn't expected, Kat didn't have to worry about keeping up her end of it.

Mrs. Darcy pulled the Tank into a gas station and got out to pump it herself. To Kat, it was like watching a flamingo mine coal. Mrs. Darcy was tall and thin with shoulder-length honey blonde hair and a long white neck that was like a slender marble pedestal for the finely sculpt-ed features of her face. She looked elegant in whatever she wore and though she moved with the quiet grace of a queen in a Hollywood movie, there was something about her that prevented her from being pretty. Mrs. Darcy was sad. The sadness clung to her like Handi-Wrap on a warm glass bowl. And even though she cooked and washed and shopped for groceries just like all the other moms, she did it through that transparent film of sadness that muted all her communications with the rest of the world.

"Kat," Mrs. Darcy said after slipping neatly back behind the wheel, "Maggie was hurt badly, but she'll probably heal fine and be back to herself before you know it. She had nightmares last night, though, and she keeps screaming out that she has to see you."

"Me?" Kat questioned. "Why?"

"I don't know why. She won't say. But I know I can count on you to calm her down some. She's always been excitable and, of course, after having had an accident, it's only natural for her to be upset. You'll be a good girl and stay with her for a little bit, won't you?" Mrs. Darcy gave Kat a quick half smile and pulled the Tank into the hospital parking lot.

"Sure," Kat replied. "Sure I will."

Maggie was on the fifth floor in the children's ward in a small room with a view of the flat, black rooftop of the building next door.

Maggie was sketching on a pad with her good arm. Her broken leg was elevated by some contraption that hung from the bed and she had a half cast on her left arm from which her skinny white fingers protruded, wiggling like worms in the sunlight.

"Hi." Kat stood at the door.

"Hey, Kat. Come on in. Is my mom with you?" Maggie dropped the pencil on the bed.

"No. She said she'd be downstairs having coffee if you needed her." Kat inched into the room, gazing at the tubes and bottles, the trays and medication charts.

"Kat," Maggie said with a pout, "you don't have to stand on the other side of the room. I don't have anything contagious, you know."

"Oh, sorry. I mean, I know you're not contagious or anything. It's just all this stuff. Doesn't that hurt?" Kat pointed to the dangling leg.

"Well, last night it really hurt a lot, but it's not too bad today. They give me stuff for the pain." Maggie seemed drained of her usual energy. Like a talking doll whose batteries were low, her words came slower and her voice was thick. Her pale skin was almost white and she looked lost among the hospital sheets. Her uncombed wispy hair was full of static electricity. It fanned out from her head like the fine strands of a web and clung to the flat pillow.

"Your mom said that you were having nightmares last night. Are you okay?"

"Nightmares?"

"Yeah. She said that you kept calling for me or something."

"Oh, that!" Maggie managed a laugh. "I couldn't sleep too much last night. My leg was killing me, my head was throbbing, and I was all alone in here. So, I pretended that I was having nightmares." Maggie paused for more breath. "You should have seen all those nurses come running when I started screaming. You know, I bet they don't do anything out there all night but chitchat. I can hear them."

"Yeah, but why were your nightmares about me?"

"They weren't about you, stupid. I just kept calling for you and saying that I had to see you. Don't you get it? You get a day out of the clutches of the Turtle and we get to spend the whole day together. Pretty brilliant, huh?"

"Wow, Maggie, I can't believe you." Kat shook her head and smiled at her injured friend. Maggie had found the means to get her own way even while tethered to a hospital bed.

Maggie dug her right elbow into the mattress and tried to shift her body more toward the center of the bed. She grimaced. "This is the pits. I hate sleeping on my back. And there's this lump right over here underneath me. Is there something stuck there?" Maggie asked, pulling at the sheets.

"Your nightgown is all balled up," Kat said, gingerly pulling it straight and smoothing out the blankets all around the bed.

Maggie lay back and closed her eyes for a few moments.

"Your mom says that you're going to be back to yourself in no time," Kat offered quietly.

Maggie turned her head toward the window, away from Kat. "That's what they tell me too, but it's not true."

"What do you mean?"

Maggie pulled the sheet up to her face and ran the edge over her eyes. She turned her head back toward Kat. "My leg will never be the same. I heard them talking outside the door last night. They must think that getting hit by a car makes you deaf or something. Anyway, I have to have some operations and I'll probably have some kind of limp for the rest of my life. And there's something else they're worried

72

about too, only I don't know what it is because a nurse came in to take my blood pressure and started blabbing away and I missed it."

"Oh, Maggie." Kat twisted the cord of her jacket around her finger and stared at the dangling leg. "It might be all right. They can probably fix the leg in an operation. And you don't know, the other thing's probably nothing. I'm sure it's nothing."

"No, they can't fix it. I heard them talking. I'm going to be some sort of freak for the rest of my life." Maggie didn't bother to turn her head this time and the tears rolled down the sides of her face.

"You won't be a freak. Really." Kat stood and walked to the window.

"Can you hand me a tissue?" Maggie asked. The tray was just out of her reach.

"Sure."

"Jeez, these things feel like cardboard," Maggie sniffed. She quickly wiped her nose and eyes with her one good hand. "You think they'd at least give you soft tissues with all the crying people do in this place. And when I have to go to the bathroom, do you know what they do? They stick this freezing cold metal bowl under me."

"Yeah, I know. My mom had those too." Kat looked out the window and watched the cars whiz by on Roosevelt Boulevard below. She really hated hospitals. "You know, my dad says that they have a lead on that car that hit you. They have parts of the license number and a good description of it."

"Big deal. They'll never find the driver." Maggie's voice was flat.

"Sure they will, Maggie. Don't you want them to get the guy that did it?"

"It wasn't a guy, Kat. It wasn't even a person. It was Twitch."

"But Maggie," Kat protested, "I saw Twitch in the window and—"

"I didn't say she did it, Kat, but she did make it happen. That curse yesterday—you wouldn't swallow the goldfish. You were sitting next to me." Maggie yawned. Her eyelids were drooping and she was struggling to stay awake. "You sat next to me."

Kat's mouth dropped. "You mean, you think that the curse somehow switched from me to you just because I was sitting next to you?"

Maggie nodded her head.

"Since when do curses jump?" Kat said, her voice rising. "I don't ever remember you mentioning that one before."

"They do," Maggie said. She raised her arm weakly and pointed to her dangling leg. "There's your evidence." Maggie closed her eyes. "You should have swallowed the goldfish," she mumbled. "You should have."

"Are you kidding? Maybe I should just leave. You look like you're getting tired anyway." Kat's face was flushed. It was always too hot in these hospital rooms.

"No. No. Don't go. Please. I'm just going to rest my eyes. Don't go, okay?" Maggie clutched the sheet up under her chin. Another tear ran down her face. "I did have nightmares last night, Kat. And I'm . . . I'm scared to be alone in this place. You probably think I'm a baby, but I can't help it. Every time I fall asleep, that car keeps hitting me, you know? I'm just reaching for the ball and then, boom, it gets me. It's like I know what's going to happen, and I want to wake up, but I'm trapped." Maggie wiped her eyes and looked up at Kat. "Don't tell anybody, okay? It's too weird."

"It's not weird," Kat said softly. "You can go to sleep. I'll stay."

"I'm afraid to go to sleep," Maggie said, the tears freely flowing down her face. "It's just going to start happening all over again."

"Why don't you just rest your eyes, then?" Kat suggested. "I'll stay as long as you want me to."

Maggie closed her eyes and was asleep within a minute.

Kat sat on the thinly padded chair in the corner and drew her knees up under her chin. The fluorescent light above her hummed. She hated everything about this place—the yellowish light, the dull green walls, and that smell, that smell they tried to hide with ammonia and detergent, but which was always there. It was the smell of hope disappearing, of fear, of unrelieved pain.

Kat held her hands over her nose, but it didn't work. The smell had wafted into her brain and awakened a host of memories that she had worked so hard to put to sleep. She could see her mother here, just like it was yesterday, hooked up to the monitors and the IVs, weakly smiling and squeezing

Kat's hand while all the life within her was dying away.

Kat swallowed the lump building in her throat and watched Maggie's restless sleep. She thought about the goldfish. She knew she couldn't have done it, even to save Maggie. She would have gagged and it wouldn't have worked. She wondered about Mrs. Twitchell. Who was she and why did she have to live in their neighborhood? Her house was a wreck, her lawn and bushes were an overgrown mess, she was so secretive that they had never seen her, and she gave them the creeps with all of her spying. Kat didn't fully believe Maggie's stories of jumping curses, goldfish cures, and witch's spells, but she had to admit that there was something very strange and weird about Twitch. And whether she caused Maggie's accident or not, Kat was sure that Maggie and the rest of the kids would be much better off if Twitch were gone.

Kat walked around to the side of Maggie's bed and listened to her light breathing. Her motionless hand with its plastic hospital bracelet was resting on the pad of paper. She had been drawing a rendition of Twitch, complete with black hat and broom. The face was contorted with a wicked grin and it almost seemed as if Twitch had somehow risen from off the paper to cast a spell on the very artist who had given her form.

Chapter
13

KAT SAT ON THE CURB across the street and stared up at Twitch's house while she waited for Paul. The sun was up but a light fog hadn't quite lifted. It clung to the bushes and wrapped itself around the damp trees. The air smelled of moist dead leaves and wet grass. With dark curtains covering every window and mist clinging to the overgrown and unkempt shrubbery, Twitch's place really did look spooky.

"Hey, Kat."

Kat jumped up. "Hey, Paul. I didn't see you coming." As they started for school, Kat took one last look at Twitch's place and made a resolution. "Did I miss anything yesterday?"

"No, just the usual. What happened with Maggie? Is she doin' okay?"

"Well, she doesn't look too good. Don't tell anybody, but her leg is messed up really bad, and she might even have some sort of limp for the rest of her life."

"No way!" Paul looked down at his feet and Kat did the same. She felt the power of her own two legs under her, how flawlessly they worked as she and Paul hurried toward school, how unconscious she had been of them before.

"Paul, we gotta get rid of Twitch. Get her out of the neighborhood, I mean."

"What are you talking about?"

"Maggie's really upset. She's convinced that this whole accident was caused by Twitch."

"Twitch? Driving a car?"

"No. She doesn't think that Twitch actually drove the car. She just thinks that Twitch somehow made the whole thing happen."

Paul made a face, and Kat decided not to mention Maggie's theory on the jumping curse. "I know it sounds weird, but you have to admit that something very strange is going on. Look at her creepy house and the fact that we have never seen her, not even once. That's just not normal. And why are her windows always covered up? And why does she watch us all the time?"

"Okay. She's weird and creepy. But how are we supposed to get rid of her?"

"I don't know exactly. Maybe we could do things like send her threatening letters, put rotten stuff around her house, burn one of her bushes or something. You know, just stuff that'll make her want to move."

"I don't know, Kat. First of all, if my dad found out about it, I'd be dead and second of all, I don't think that kind of stuff will scare Twitch away."

"Do you have any better suggestions?"

"No," Paul answered slowly. "But what's the big deal about getting rid of her anyway?"

"Look, Paul, Maggie's all messed up in the hospital and she'll never be the same and when she gets out of the hospital, she'll have to move right back in next to Twitch again. You don't know what it's like to live next to some creep who spies on your every move. It drives Maggie crazy and I just think she deserves a break. I don't care what anyone says, I'm going to do it."

They walked along in silence, crunching the dried leaves beneath their feet, and she knew that he was thinking it over. Paul was a very deliberate sort of person. He never raised his hand in class unless he was absolutely sure of the answer, and he took forever making his move in checkers or deciding which property to buy in Monopoly.

She would never forget him that night of her mother's viewing. She had stood beside the casket, numb and empty, while old relatives and people she didn't even know came up and shook her hand or kissed her cheek. "I'm sorry, I'm so sorry," they all said. She couldn't smile or cry or even nod hello. So she just stood, stuck to her spot like a freshly cut tree stump. All the living, feeling part of her had been lopped off, but her feet remained rooted to the carpet to the left of the casket.

It was all so unreal, so like a dream. She saw people's

mouths opening and closing and heard words come out, but nothing made any sense. Everything moved in a sort of slow-motion fog. And then she saw Paul. He was alone and was peeking around the corner into the room. He got in the line that snaked its way up toward the casket. Three times, just as he got toward the front, he abruptly left. Then a few minutes later, there he would be in the back of the line again, winding his way around the room. He kept his hands in his pockets and his eyes on the floor. It gave Kat something to do, watching him and wondering if he was going to make it, and it made her feel sorry for someone besides herself.

He made it to the front on his fourth try. All he said was "Hey, Kat" and he gave her a quick, sympathetic look. But that was all she needed. Besides Maggie, he was her only friend to come that night.

"Hey, Kat," Paul said, interrupting her thoughts, "aren't you going to salute back?"

They were approaching Patton Circle. The General was standing at attention, his hand rigidly pressed to his forehead. It looked as though he were saluting the traffic light.

Even Paul didn't understand about the General. "Lay off of him, Paul," Kat said. "He's just an old man."

"Yeah, a really weird one."

The light changed and the General relaxed his stance. He began talking in an animated fashion and waving his arms.

"Does he want you or something?" Paul asked. "What's he doing?"

"No. He doesn't see me. It's kind of hard to explain, but he doesn't notice the same things other people do. We'd have to go over to talk to him."

"Forget it."

"I don't mean now. Let's just get going. I don't want to be stuck with detention again for being late."

Chapter

14

AT 3:15 EVERYONE IN THE CLASS was sitting silently, hands folded on desks. It hadn't been a good day. Marty Kologinski got caught spitting out the window on the public school kids who came occasionally when they had half days to taunt the Catholics still stuck in school. Tyler Reid had a water gun in his desk, which he had used successfully all morning, mostly against Kat and her friends. But as everyone filed back in from lunch, he missed his target and sprayed the blackboard. A long dark streak slowly made its way down a math problem, smearing fractions, severing equations.

"This will be the last opportunity for the guilty party to step forward." Sister Mildred was placing her pencils and pens in the top drawer of the desk and loading up her black book bag.

The class remained quiet.

"All right. You will write out every word in chapters five through ten of your vocabulary workbook with their definitions. You will do it tonight and have it on my desk tomorrow morning."

There was a collective groan as the students reached under their desks to pull out their books.

"Quiet!" Sister Mildred slapped her ruler on the desk. She was in one of her moods. "Kathryn O'Connor."

"Yes, Sister?" Kat looked up.

"You will remain after school today."

"But, Sister, I didn't—"

"Enough," the nun said sharply. "There will be no discussion of the matter. You will stay."

Kat glared at Tyler, but he certainly wasn't the hero type. He pretended to be busy loading his backpack and kept his eyes glued to his books.

Paul shot her a sympathetic look. When the bell rang, he stopped at her desk on the way out. "You want me to tell your dad where you are?"

"Yeah. Thanks." Kat rested her chin in her hand. "How could she think it was me? I can't believe it. Tyler is such a creep."

"Are you going to tell?"

"Of course I'm not going to tell." Kat kicked the desk in front of her. "Just beat up Tyler for me on the way home, okay?"

Paul smiled. "Yeah, sure."

He left and the room became uncomfortably quiet. Sister Mildred stared down at Kat across the empty aisles.

"Kathryn," Sister said, "come up and carry my book bag. We're going to the convent."

"The convent?"

"Yes. And bring your things."

Kat had never been in the convent before in all her eight years at the school. There was a locked windowless door at the end of the hall on the second floor that all the sisters used to come to school in the mornings and to go home in the afternoons. Students were not allowed. At least, Kat had never seen any kids enter there. Spraying a blackboard with a water pistol wasn't that terrible of a thing, even if she had done it.

Sister fumbled for her keys and the door squeaked open. They entered what looked like a living room. It was a large area with wooden floors and a few very thin area rugs. The furniture looked old-fashioned and unused. The air was cool and had a faint sweet smell, like rose petals in water. Kat was surprised. Other than the crucifixes and the large color picture of the Pope on the wall, it looked like a regular room that one of her older neighbors would live in. She had expected something darker, like cubicles and rough-hewn wooden tables. She had seen a movie once where the monks had lived like that.

"Take a seat in the corner over there, Kathryn. You can put my book bag beside the table."

Kat did as she was told. At least there were no instruments of torture lying about, she thought to herself.

Sister Mildred eased herself onto the hard couch. "Kathryn, do you know the pigeon man who feeds the birds on Patton Circle?"

"The pigeon man?" Kat stammered. "I, I know who he is."

"Do you talk to him?"

"I've talked to him, but Sister, he's not really a bad person or anything . . ."

"How often do you talk to him?" Sister Mildred stared unblinkingly at Kat. Her eyes were very small and surrounded by puffy skin. You couldn't even tell what color they were.

Kat hesitated.

"Kathryn, it's all right. Just tell me how often you speak with him."

"Well, just about every day. Every school day, anyway. I just stop for a little bit on my way home. He's not dangerous or anything."

"I want you to do me a favor. Do you call him 'the General'?"

Kat nodded her head in wonder.

"I've been giving the General food and old clothes and things for many years. Lately, however, he won't come to get them. I've been to his home several times, but he won't take what I bring."

"He has a home?!" Kat blurted out. She had always assumed that the General slept on the bench in the circle.

"It's a house on Jackson Street over in St. Bernard's parish. He doesn't spend much time there. It's in terrible disrepair. I do think that he sleeps there most nights, though. At least, he used to. Anyway, I've even tried, on my good days, dropping some things off at the circle, but he refuses to even speak with me."

"He probably thinks you're the enemy." Kat had seen

the General act this way with strangers who unknowingly invaded the circle.

"Something like that." Sister Mildred leaned forward. "I'm going to bring a small bag of things to school every couple of days or so and I would like you to take them to the General."

"Sure, I'll take them to him."

"Good girl. Come with me to the kitchen then."

Kat followed Sister Mildred down a short hall to the kitchen. Sister John, dressed in her habit and a pair of fuzzy blue slippers, was standing at the counter chopping onions. She smiled at Kat.

Sister Mildred filled a small shopping bag with crackers, cheese, and a few boxed items taken from a tall metal cabinet. She handed it to Kat and led her to the front door of the convent. Kat hesitated before going out. "I guess, then, you didn't ever think that I was the one with the water pistol?"

"No, dear. You have your failings, but shooting classmates with a water pistol is not one of them."

"Oh." Kat turned to leave, wondering what her other failings were.

"And Kathryn, you might want to tell Mr. Reid to leave his pistol at home from now on." The nun winked at her. "It will save us all a lot of grief."

Kat almost dropped the bag. "You knew all the time?"

"I may be old, but I'm not blind, dear."

"But why did you let him get away with it?"

"Did he get away with it?" Sister Mildred had this

annoying tendency to answer questions with questions. But she was right. Everyone would be seriously down on Tyler for ruining their night with extra homework.

"But why do the rest of us have to suffer for him?"

"A little bit of constructive suffering will do you good. You, for one, can use the extra work to help with your grades. Good-bye, Kathryn, and thank you." Sister Mildred shut the door.

Kat stood staring at the door for a few moments in disbelief. "I don't need any constructive suffering," she said through clenched teeth to the closed door. She turned and walked slowly down the steps. What did Sister Mildred know about her life and what was good for her? Nothing. Kat glanced back at the stone convent as she waited to cross Battersby Street. She'd bring the food to the General as promised, for his sake, but she wasn't going back into that convent again.

Kat shifted the bag in her arms as she walked up Cottman Avenue. She just couldn't imagine the gentle, confused General in his pigeon-stained overcoat visiting in the convent parlor, or the self-righteous Sister Mildred propped up on the bench at Patton Circle. They were like polar ends of a magnet, like Heidi and Attila the Hun, like the scatterbrained Scarecrow and the Wicked Witch of the West. Kat wondered how they ever came to know each other.

The afternoon was fading. She quickened her steps toward Patton Circle.

Chapter
15

"REQUEST PERMISSION to advance, sir." Kat stepped up onto the circle and saluted.

"Advance. Advance." The General sat slumped on the wooden bench.

"I brought some supplies, General." Kat put the bag beside him and opened it up, pulling out the boxes. "See? There's bread, crackers, cheese. Good stuff."

The General fingered the bag of bread suspiciously. "These are not your usual rations. I hope that these were not stolen from the civilian population. I would hate to see you court martialed, soldier. I would hate to lose you," he said sternly.

"No, sir. It's really okay. There were extras in the mess tent and the cook let me have them. It would just go to waste if we didn't eat it. I thought maybe you might want some of it."

"A dishonorable discharge is a stain, you know. A black stain." The General pulled a piece of bread out of its plastic wrapper and began to slowly chew. The pigeons waddled toward him and hopped up onto the bench, expecting to receive their share. But the General didn't seem to notice. He just stared straight ahead. A few birds fluttered onto his lap and pecked the bread right out of his motionless hand.

Kat twisted the plastic bag shut and put it with the other food. "You okay, General?" She noticed that his hair was wet with perspiration and that he had a large purple bruise on the right side of his forehead, just below the hairline. "Maybe you should see the medic. I think you might be getting sick. And you seem to be wounded too." Kat lifted her hand to touch the bruise on his forehead, but the General jerked away, suddenly animated, and jumped to his feet.

"Him! Him! Help him first! Over there!" The General was pointing, arm rigid and eyes wide. Then just as quickly, he hugged his arms to his body and collapsed on the bench, weeping.

Kat moved toward him carefully and gently stroked his shoulder. "It's okay, General. It's okay."

He wiped his face across his dirty sleeve and looked up at her. "We're alone," he whispered confidentially. "No one believes us. They're against us, all of them. Surrounded. That's what they've done. They've got us surrounded. We must hold our position. Dig in." The General began to point and give orders to the shadows around him and suddenly the little traffic island seemed peopled with a phantom army, fighting ghosts whose souls could not sleep, but rose to the call of their General, digging their trenches, cocking their weapons, forming an invincible line against the ever-present enemy. Kat closed her eyes and tried to see them too. She imagined the row houses gone and in their place fields of cold mud. Beyond loomed ancient dark forests and crumbling villages, an enemy behind every tree. She shivered.

The General fell silent. He had overexerted himself and was panting for air. Kat leaned over him and tried to get the attention of his vacant eyes. "General, you just take a short break and I'll watch over the troops for you," she said softly.

The General cocked his head and squinted at her, then crumpled back against the bench. "You're a good soldier, Kat," he said with a sigh.

She took one of his old jackets off the ground and rolled it up at the end of the bench. "Here, put your head here, General."

The General lay down on the hard wooden bench. He took Kat's hand and squeezed it tightly. His skin was hot. "They're all around us, soldier, coming closer," he whispered. "Don't surrender. Don't ever surrender, Kat."

Kat stood there with him for a few minutes until his eyes closed and his grip loosened. She hadn't dared pull herself away for fear that he would have been jolted back into another battle. She rolled up the paper bag as best she could to keep the pigeons out and put it on the bench at his feet. "Goodnight, General," she whispered, and the sea of pigeons parted before her as she left the circle.

The sunlight was fading behind a bank of gray clouds, and the shadows were beginning to gather in the alleys and under the porches as she made her way home. There was a low rumbling of thunder in the distance and the air smelled of rain.

Chapter
16

WHEN KAT GOT IN, the house smelled like fried onions and she went straight to the kitchen. Her dad and brother were sitting at the old square formica table eating steak sandwiches. It was such an ugly table. The top of it was pea green and there were little flecks of yellow running through it. It used to belong to her grandmother. When she died, Kat's mother had taken it. Kat hated how that stupid table was still sitting there in their house and her mother and grandmother were gone.

"Well?" Her father looked up from his sandwich. "What happened this time?"

"Nothing happened, Dad. It wasn't my fault. Sister Mildred made me stay after school but I didn't do anything."

"You didn't do anything?" He looked at her skeptically, his glass of milk suspended between the table and his lips.

"Dad, I didn't. Really. It was all a big mistake."

"Okay, Kat, if you say so." He gave her a half smile, but she knew he didn't believe her. She'd been in trouble at school too much this year. He pushed his half-eaten sandwich away from his place and replaced it with a magazine. He flipped through the pages slowly, not lingering long enough to read any one story.

She wanted to tell him what had happened, but she couldn't. He had told her weeks ago to stay away from the General and she hadn't listened to him. He was already concerned about her dropping grades and her chronic lateness. Now he would probably think that she had turned to lying, too. Kat opened her mouth, but there was nothing she could say to make it better. She felt a tightness in her chest and turned away. She went into the living room and threw herself into her favorite armchair.

He just didn't understand. No one did. She couldn't go back to being the same person she was before. The whole world was different and she seemed to be the only one who noticed it. There was her mother on the mantel, flat and lifeless, trapped behind glass, screwed into a picture frame. It was as if she had never even existed. Her father just kept on churning out those stupid manuals. Danny still laughed at Looney Tunes and tried to get his milk to come out his nose. The people across the street, who had seemed so sad at the funeral, had had a Fourth of July party the very next day! She had lain there in bed and listened to firecrackers and singing and loud laughing late into the night. It was like everyone paused for just that one day and said, "Oh, we're so very sorry" and then forgot all about it and went on with their lives as if nothing had happened. And if they thought that she could just go to school and take math tests and try out for the basketball team and laugh at stupid jokes as if nothing had changed from last year, they were wrong.

It was like they had been on a long car trip and her mother had fallen out somewhere along the way. Everyone else just kept right on playing the radio, checking the maps, and admiring the scenery. She felt like shaking them all and making them notice. The vacation was over. The fun was gone. She wanted to get out of the car.

She heard her father's chair push back against the floor and she jumped and ran up to her room.

Chapter

17

"KAT, DADDY SAYS THAT you have to get downstairs right now." Danny burst into her room. She had been lying in the dark and he was flicking the light switch on and off.

"Knock it off, Danny."

"Right now, Kat. You better get up." He was still flicking the lights.

"Danny, I said knock it off." Kat put a pillow over face.

"I'm telling. Daddy, she isn't coming. Daddy. . ." Danny clumped off down the stairs, but his shrill voice lingered after him and she could hear him gleefully tattling below.

When she came down they were putting on their coats. "Where are you going?"

"Kat, honey, I told you last week that I was going to that baseball card show at the convention center. Remember?" He leaned down to zip up Danny's jacket.

"He's going with you?"

"Yes." Mr. O'Connor stuck his hands in his pockets and fished for his keys.

"I like baseball cards," Kat said. She had a collection of cards that she used to care about in a binder under her bed.

"I know you do, but I'm going with Owen O'Hara, my contact at Weston Electronics. He has a little boy Danny's age, and he set this whole thing up."

"But Danny doesn't know a baseball from a bottle cap."

"I do too, stupid." Danny stuck his tongue out at her.

"Kat, it's a business thing, okay? If it's any good, maybe you and I can go back again this weekend. There's some sandwich steak in the refrigerator you can fry up and I left your roll on the counter."

He turned toward her before going out the door and she thought he might hug her goodbye. But he only picked a small loose thread off the front of her sweater and gently pushed her hair back from out of her eyes. "Don't forget, if you have any problems, just give Mrs. Olshefski a call." They went out the door and Kat locked it behind them.

She didn't really like being alone in the house at night. There were always lots of creaks and groans that she never heard during the day. When the sun fell and her father was gone, it was as though the house in some sense came alive and was trying to stretch its aching walls and shift its cramped floors from beneath the confines of paint and paper and nails and rugs. And the darkness outside seemed like a great ocean pressing up against the windows, seeping under the doors and flooding into the basement. She felt like it could come crashing in on her at any minute and she would be washed out into that great vast blackness.

Kat went right to the phone to call Maggie. Even the light sound of her footsteps seemed to echo through the empty house. It was weird how something invisible like silence could feel so heavy and press in all around you. Maggie's voice would push it back. Kat snatched up the receiver and dialed. She couldn't wait to see how Maggie was feeling and to fill her in on Sister Mildred and the General. She cradled the receiver on her shoulder and counted the rings on the other end of the line. Finally, she heard a thin 'hello.'

"Hi, Mrs. Darcy. It's Kat. Can I talk to Maggie?"

"I'm sorry, Kat, but the doctor is here right now and Maggie's awfully tired. Maybe you could try calling back tomorrow."

"Oh," Kat said. She had been wrapping the phone cord around her finger and the tip of her pinky was bright red. "Okay," she said slowly. "Could you tell her I said hi?"

"I will, honey. Thanks for calling."

Kat hung up the phone and the silence flooded back into the room. She walked around the downstairs pulling the blinds and shutting the curtains on the picture window. She went into the cold kitchen to make her sandwich. The stove top was still splattered with grease from last week's dinner. The utensils lay scattered on the counter. There were crayons and pencils in with the silverware and the potatoes in the pantry closet had long white sprouts growing out of them. They weren't supposed to eat in the living room, but she couldn't bring herself to sit in that silent, lifeless kitchen all alone.

It was almost like the kitchen had died along with her mother. It never gave off those great smells anymore of a stuffed chicken or cherry pie or alphabet soup. The teakettle sat unused on the back burner, a layer of dust covering its lid. It was only after her mother died that Kat realized that it wasn't so much the tea that she had liked, but the event of drinking it with her mother. It didn't taste good to her at all now, no matter how much sugar she put in.

Kat sat cross-legged in the green armchair and put her plate in her lap. She flipped through the channels halfheartedly. There was never much on at dinner time. Her father still refused to unblock MTV from their cable. Thirteen years old and she had to choose between CNN and the Cartoon Network.

Kat had just taken the first bite of her sandwich when something caught her eye. Quickly, she flipped back two stations. She couldn't believe it! Without thinking, Kat rose out of her chair and the plate fell clattering to the floor. There filling the screen was a picture of Maggie Darcy, her best friend.

Chapter
18

MAGGIE'S PICTURE was on the local six o'clock news. It looked like her seventh-grade school portrait. Kat moved closer to the television and raised the volume. The anchorman was reporting that there had been a break in the case. A suspect in the hit-and-run had been arrested.

"Yes!" Kat said aloud and pumped her fist in the air. The suspect's name was Douglas Ellison and the television cut away to a reporter on the scene. The camera panned the area outside the Roundhouse, the old circular police building on Race Street, where bystanders, reporters, and photographers were all milling about. Suddenly the crowd parted and two burly police officers in uniform led the suspect toward the doors. Lights from the television cameras flooded over him and he squinted.

Kat gasped. "It has to be a mistake," she mumbled. Her

eyes stung with the surprise and a wave of nausea swept over her. She sat on the edge of the coffee table, her hands crossed over her mouth. The suspect being led away, being buffeted by the howls of the crowd, was the General.

His eyes were wide and darting all around, like those of a small child cornered by his tormentors in the school yard. Beads of perspiration ran down the sides of his face. Bystanders shouted at him. Newspeople pushed microphones in his face. His hands were cuffed behind his back and police officers were trying to move him forward through the crowd. Someone spit at him. Kat put her hands on the screen, but she couldn't shield him. It was like watching a caged sparrow being poked at with a stick.

The newsman reported how a tip from one of the victim's neighbors had led to the suspect's arrest. The camera zoomed in on his face. "According to police spokesperson Janet Beans there has been no confession. As a matter of fact, the suspect refuses to talk at all other than to give his name, rank, and serial number." The reporter smirked at the camera. "Back to you, Larry."

Kat flipped off the television. She had wanted the police to catch the driver who had hit Maggie and lock him up forever. But not the General. He was just a harmless old man. Kat couldn't even imagine him driving a car. Even if he had done it, he probably didn't know he did. Now Maggie was really going to think that the accident was Kat's fault. Not only had Kat refused to swallow the goldfish, but she kept up her friendship with the General despite Maggie's warnings of doom.

She wondered if Maggie knew about the arrest and she

thought of her friend as she had left her in the hospital, sad and drained of energy. If the General was the villain, Kat thought, then she should hate him. But the image of his terrified face would not leave her. She knew that he wouldn't know what was happening to him, that he would think he was a prisoner of war. Could she go visit him at the jail? But she didn't even know where that was. She wanted to call the judge to explain about the General, how he was different, but she didn't know who to call. Everyone would think that she was a traitor if she tried to help the person who ran over her very best friend. No one knew the General so no one would understand. They all just thought that he was a loony old man. No one knew him like she did, except maybe . . . Sister Mildred! She ran to the closet and threw on her coat. She would go back to the convent and get Sister Mildred to help her.

Kat slammed the door and quickly jumped down the steps to the sidewalk. The wind had picked up considerably and the trees were bowing before it. They bent under each gust then mournfully rose, their slender branches reaching desperately for the drying leaves that the wind had torn from them. The trees clattered together in confusion and dismay while their offspring skittered away, scraping noisily against the sidewalk and the asphalt street.

Kat noticed Twitch staring down at her from the second-floor window. She didn't even bother to cross the street. She just didn't care anymore. She stood at the edge of the grass, glared at the witch, and spit with the wind. She started to run to the convent. She ran without stopping, darting recklessly into streets, flinging herself forward against the wind, pushing hard, until it seemed the ground gave way before her and she was part of the night itself.

She was at the convent door sweating, panting for breath, her hair wild and tangled from the wind. She rang the doorbell rapidly five or six times and heard its muted buzz from somewhere within. Sister Dolores answered. She stood in the doorway, hands on hips. The kids all referred to Sister Dolores as the Sarge. She was a large, angular woman with a jutting jaw that always seemed clenched in anger. She had a marked dislike for children, especially the seventh- and eighth-graders, and she was suspicious of everything they did.

"What do you want?"

"I have to see Sister Mildred right away!" Kat puffed.

"Is she expecting you?"

"No, Sister, but it's really important. I have to see her. You have to let me in."

"I'm sorry, but the Sisters are at prayer. You should have called first. Does your mother know you are here?" Sister Dolores held onto the handle of the screen door defensively.

"I don't have a mother," Kat shouted. "I know nobody around here has noticed it, but she's dead! Dead, dead, dead. See? I said it. She's dead. So just let me in."

"Listen, young lady, if you think that that kind of brazen behavior is going to get you anywhere, you're wrong. Now you just turn yourself around and march home to your parents before I make you sorry you were ever born." Sister Dolores began to close the door.

"No, wait! Sister Mildred! Sister Mildred!" Kat

frantically called into the convent before the door slammed shut on her.

She sat on the top step in the darkness, her chin in her hands, and watched the rolling black clouds. They were moving quickly in the strong wind and seemed to be tumbling one upon the other in a frantic attempt to get away from whatever lurked beyond the horizon.

A crack of light appeared on the step. The convent door had reopened slightly and Sister Mildred peered out. "Kathryn, come in here."

Kat jumped up and went inside. It was warm and quiet.

"She wouldn't let me in. I had to see you. The General. . ."

Sister Mildred put her finger to her lips. "The Sisters are at prayer. Come with me." The nun led the way down a long empty hallway and turned left into a small bedroom. There was barely enough space to turn around. This was much more like the monastic living quarters that Kat had imagined she would find in a convent. To the right of the door was a single bed with a plain wooden headboard and a light blue spread. A small desk and chair sat opposite it. The walls were off-white and were decorated with religious ornaments and pictures of saints. It was impeccably neat and ruthlessly organized.

"Sit." Sister Mildred motioned Kat to the bed. She closed the door and pulled out the desk chair. She sat facing Kat. "Now, what is all this commotion about?"

"Did you see the General on the news?"

The nun nodded her head slowly.

"Can't we do something to get him out of jail?" Kat asked.

"No. I'm afraid not. He's been arrested for a serious crime and the judge will most likely set a high bail. If you can't post your bail, you can't get out. That's the law. The General has very little money."

"But, Sister, it's not like he's a criminal or anything," Kat complained.

"Kat, he hit Maggie with his car and drove off. That's a crime and it makes him a criminal in the eyes of the law."

"But how could it have been him? I never even saw him in a car. How could somebody like him drive?"

"He's had a car for many years, Kat. I'm sure that his license and registration have long since expired, but that doesn't mean that he doesn't drive. I agree that someone like him should never be behind the wheel, but there isn't much we can do about it. Years ago, back when he was a little more rational, I tried to get him to sell the car or at least give me the keys. He wouldn't do it. He could never see or admit that he was losing the ability to drive. Now, he's too far gone for me to reason with at all. It's just a tragedy."

"All right, but even if he did do it, he probably didn't know that he did it. And he sure doesn't understand why they arrested him. Somebody spit on him, did you see that? Can't we call the judge or something and explain what the General's like? And he's sick, too. When I stopped this afternoon to give him that stuff, he was real hot and all sweaty."

"No. We can't call the judge. The city will give the

General a lawyer to help him in court and I've already put a call in to find out who that will be. I'll do what I can, but I'm afraid that there's just not much we can do to help him."

"Great. So we're just going to sit around and do nothing and let him have a heart attack in jail or something." Kat picked at a small pull in the bedspread.

"I am praying for him."

"Yeah, and a lot of good that'll do," Kat said under her breath. She had prayed so hard for her mother that the words of the Hail Mary used to constantly buzz around inside her head like the melody of a popular song played too often on the radio. And it hadn't helped at all.

Sister Mildred fingered the silver crucifix that hung around her neck, but said nothing.

"Forget it," Kat said. "I better go." She slid off the bed and stood by the door, her hand on the knob. "Who cares, anyway? I'm sorry I bothered you."

The nun didn't move. She stared at Kat with her small puffy eyes.

There were voices and footsteps out in the hall. Prayers were apparently over and the nuns were moving throughout the house. Somebody began to poke out a tune on a piano. Sister Mildred put her finger to her lips again and motioned Kat to return to her seat on the bed. Kat hesitated. She wanted to go. Sister Mildred wasn't going to do anything to help and Kat didn't want to stick around for any lectures. Besides, it was too hot in the little cubicle and it was making her sick to her stomach. She couldn't believe that she had come here in the first place.

Sister Mildred furrowed her forehead and pointed to the bed again. "Kat, sit down."

"I don't want to." Kat had never openly defied Sister Mildred before and she braced herself for the consequences.

"Kathryn," the nun said in a softer voice, "if you don't sit down, I'll have to sic Sister Dolores on you."

Kat released her grip on the knob and smiled involuntarily. But she didn't sit.

"Kathryn," the nun said slowly, "do you know how the police were able to catch the General?"

"The license number, I guess," Kat answered. "Paul saw part of it and they probably just figured out the rest." Kat was standing at the foot of Sister Mildred's bed, examining the plaques and religious ornaments arranged on a small shelf on the wall. She looked up just in time to see a self-satisfied look flash across the nun's face.

"It was you!" Kat blurted out. "Wasn't it? You were the one who turned him in. No wonder you didn't want to help!"

"Watch your tone, young lady," the nun said sharply.

"Can I just go home now?" Kat asked through her teeth.

"No. I'm not through yet."

Kat slumped against the wall. She was suddenly very tired.

"It wasn't me," Sister Mildred said in a softer tone, "but whoever turned him in did the right thing. I just wanted you to know that before you left."

"Yeah, sure," Kat sighed. Her eyes rested on the saintly statues on the shelf, their perfect faces upturned and etched with looks of devotion and faith. She longed to be like them, so sure in their beliefs and so empty of anger.

Kat straightened up suddenly. She picked up a small black-and-white photo that had fallen flat on the back of the shelf behind Saint Francis of Assisi. It was an old picture of two guys and a girl at the beach. The girl, who was standing in the middle, had long hair that reached almost to her knees. But it was the guy on the left that Kat focused on. She held the picture close to her face.

"It's him!" Kat said. "Isn't it? This is the General!" Kat held the picture out toward Sister Mildred. "Is that you in the middle?"

The nun took the picture from Kat and stared down at it for several moments without speaking.

"I took the picture," she finally said.

"Is the General your brother or was he your . . ." Kat was thinking the word "boyfriend," but she wasn't sure if that was an appropriate thing to say to an aging nun.

Sister Mildred fingered the faded photo. "No," she said, after a long pause, "we're not related."

Kat stood silently, staring toward the picture, hoping for more of an explanation.

"Kat," Sister Mildred asked, "why do you care about the General?"

"I don't know," Kat answered slowly. "I just do."

Sister Mildred shifted on the hard chair.

"You know," Kat said, taking a seat on the bed, "there was a sparrow once that flew into our kitchen by mistake when I opened the door. It just kept fluttering all around, smashing into the window, looking for a way out. And I could just feel how frightened it was. It was so desperate and frantic and confused. When I saw the General tonight on television, it made me feel the same way. I just wish we could do something to help him."

The nun shook her head.

"But if you've known him so long, you must know how to contact his family or somebody. They could get him money for bail. You just can't leave him in jail."

"Kathryn, things aren't as simple as you want them to be." Sister Mildred placed the old photograph on her lap and stared at the three happy young people, frozen in time, smiling at the future. "You're right, of course. This is the General on the left. That's how he used to look before all the trouble began."

"The trouble?" Kat asked.

Sister Mildred paused, then looked intently at Kat. "Kathryn, since you seem to care so much about him, I'll tell you a few things about the General's life. It's not a happy story, but maybe it will help you understand his situation and why there's not too much we can do to help him." The nun sighed and settled back in her chair.

Chapter
19

"I FIRST MET THE GENERAL In the summer of 1942. I had just completed my first year of college and I took a job down the shore, on the boardwalk in Atlantic City. It was different then, before the casinos, charming and beautiful. I shared a few rooms with my sister, Julia, in an old house a few blocks from the beach."

"Julia!" Kat exclaimed. "The transparent lady. The General talks to her all the time. Is she the one in the picture?"

"Yes. Julia worked in an ice-cream parlor around the corner from our house. It was there that she met Michael Ellison."

"There's a pigeon named Mr. Ellison," Kat interrupted again. "It's the General's favorite one. Do you think he named it after him?"

"Perhaps. In any case, Julia and Michael began to spend

all their time together. As I recall, it was a very hot summer. Whenever they had a day off, they would lie on the beach all day, dashing down to cool off in the waves when the heat became too much. At night, they stayed up on the boardwalk to get the breeze off the ocean, and strolled from one end to the other. They used to bring me home a bag of soft pretzels or a dripping ice-cream sandwich. About halfway through the summer, Michael's older brother, Douglas, came down from the city to join him."

"The General?" Kat asked.

"Yes," the nun answered. "Only, he wasn't the General then. He was just Douglas. Julia fixed it up that everywhere she and Michael would go, Douglas and I would be invited."

"You mean, you, like, dated him?" Kat asked.

"Well, Douglas and I were more like friends. It became obvious to me within a few weeks that Douglas was falling very much in love with Julia."

"But I thought Michael loved her," Kat said.

"He did. It seems that they both did. Julia was a special sort of person. She had thick wavy black hair that hung all the way down her back and she had beautiful ivory skin. But mostly, it was her exuberance that attracted people. Nothing was ordinary to her. She was wild and excitable. When you were with her, you felt like you were discovering the world for the first time. She could find romance in the smell of the wet boardwalk after a summer rain and beauty in the broken shells on the beach. She threw her whole soul into everything that she did and she was totally happy that summer."

"Did she know they both loved her?" Kat asked.

"I think she did, but she never said anything. It was obvious she cared only for Michael. By the end of the summer, Julia and Michael were engaged."

"Did they get married?" Kat asked.

"Well, I don't know if you keep up with your history lessons or not, but there was a war going on. Michael and Douglas had both volunteered to fight. Just about all the young men in the country were going off to war. Michael and Douglas were in the same company and they were required to report for basic training the first week of September. So, when the summer ended, they left us and we went back to the city to our parents' house, me to begin my second year of college and Julia to work behind the counter in Wanamakers. She did nothing that year but dream of Michael and stroll the department store floors picking out the things that she wanted for her house when she was married. And then one day the letter came."

"Oh, no," Kat whispered.

"Michael was dead."

"Was he shot?"

"No. I wish he had been. It seems that Michael and Douglas were out in a jeep bringing supplies back to their encampment in North Africa. Douglas was driving. Apparently both of them had been drinking. In any case, the jeep overturned. Douglas was thrown free and was relatively unharmed, but Michael was crushed and died on the spot."

"Oh, wow," Kat said. "What did Julia do?"

"Well, she was devastated. She blamed Douglas. She said very many cruel things to him."

"Did she think that he did it on purpose?" Kat asked.

"I think that she accused him of that, yes. Douglas was dishonorably discharged and sent home. He came to our house and begged Julia to hear him out. She would have nothing to do with him. Sometimes, he would sit for hours outside on the steps in front of our house. Julia didn't care. She felt he deserved his misery. She was more than miserable herself. She filled her life with sadness in the same way that she had filled it with joy before the tragedy. She wore black. She wouldn't eat. She quit her job. And then one night, she took our parents' car, parked it on the middle of the Tacony-Palmyra bridge, climbed up on the rail, and just let herself go."

"You mean she killed herself?" Kat asked incredulously.

Sister Mildred paused. "It was a terrible thing to do. She was just a girl of such extremes. She acted on impulses. I often think of her flying through the night air, arms outstretched, and I'm sure that she felt no fear, no regrets. In happier days, she was like the sun itself. In sadness, she just rushed to be a part of the darkness."

"Wow," Kat said. "What did the General . . . I mean Douglas do?"

"Well, he pretty much just gave up on life altogether. He never went back to school. He lived off his parents for a long time. He took odd jobs here and there, but he never amounted to anything."

"How did he get a car? I mean, the one that he hit Maggie with?" Kat asked.

"When his parents died, they left him their house and whatever money they may have had. He has lived, or I should say, existed there, ever since. His mind has slowly degenerated over the years. He has no friends or family that I know of."

"Except for the pigeons," Kat said. "And you."

"Well, yes, I suppose," the nun answered. "And now, my story is finished. I've told you more than I meant to." Sister Mildred stared silently at the old photograph for a few moments. Kat tried to catch the expression on her face, but Sister Mildred's head was bent low. When she looked up, the young girl who had spent the summer in Atlantic City was gone and the old Sister Mildred was back.

"Let's go. It's getting late, young lady, and you need to be getting home."

Kat left the convent just as the rain was beginning. She didn't run this time, but walked slowly, immersing herself in the torrents, ignoring the cold sting of the drops as they ran through her hair and dripped from her fingertips.

She wished that they would wash her away to a different country where she could start all over again, a new person. Tyler and his friends were going to crucify her tomorrow over the General's arrest, and she wasn't looking forward to it.

Chapter
20

AT NIGHT, WHILE SHE WAS DREAMING, the rain came
again. It washed her out of bed, down streets, and toward
the river. She wasn't afraid, but floated peacefully on
her back in the cool water, and slid joyfully into the
choppy dark water of the Delaware. She splashed in and
out, magically, like a dolphin, until she saw her mother
waving at her from far below. She began to dive down to
her, descending farther and farther, but no matter how far
she went, she just couldn't seem to reach her. Suddenly, Kat
realized that she couldn't breathe. She turned and lunged for
the surface, but she couldn't make it. Horrified, she saw that
Julia was floating beside her, her long hair flowing out
behind her like so much tangled seaweed, and she started
pulling Kat down. Kat was choking, struggling, gasping
for air.

Kat woke with a start. She jumped out of bed, opened

her bedroom window, and stuck her head out into the cool morning air. She took several long, deep breaths. Her hands were trembling and she felt sick to her stomach. She just couldn't go to school today. She sat on the edge of her bed and tried to think of an appropriate illness. Jennifer McLaughlin had had the chicken pox last week. They were probably going around. She checked in the mirror, hopeful that there would be some telltale red spots, but she saw none. Just the beginnings of a pimple on her chin. She'd have to try for the upset stomach. She sat on the floor for a few minutes and rested her head against the cast-iron radiator in the hope that it would temporarily raise her temperature. Feeling sufficiently flushed, she padded down the steps in her bedroom slippers and nightgown to the kitchen.

"Kat, why aren't you dressed?" Mr. O'Connor was at the table drinking his morning coffee.

"I think I better stay home. I don't feel too well." Kat collapsed into a chair and put her hand on her stomach.

"Kat, don't start this."

"But, Dad, really, I don't feel good."

"All right, come here, let me feel your head." Kat leaned down to him and Mr. O'Connor put his cool, smooth hand over her forehead. He had long fine fingers, and he still wore his wedding ring on his left hand. She could hear it clink as he drummed his fingers on the table. "Kathryn, there is absolutely nothing wrong with you. You're fine. Now go get ready for school."

"But I don't feel fine, Dad. Really, I think I'm coming down with something."

"Kathryn, I really don't want to go through this today,"

he sighed. "You have to go to school. There's no getting around it."

Kat's eyes filled with tears, but she turned quickly away.

Mr. O'Connor stood and went after her. "Kat, wait." He put his arms on her shoulders. "Did you know the collar of this robe is all turned in?" He gently pulled the material out and smoothed it down. "I was just thinking, how about if Danny and I drive you in today?"

"No, it's okay. I can walk," Kat mumbled and headed for the stairs.

It was true that she had faked sickness quite a bit these last few months, but it wasn't a lie to say that she didn't feel right. There wasn't any one particular part of her body that hurt. It was just this overall sluggish feeling she had as if she had fallen into a great vat of molasses and it was hardening around her.

She climbed the stairs slowly. She was going to have to go to school. The very thought of facing all those kids' "I told you so's" on the day after the General's arrest was wreaking havoc on her insides. Her stomach was flipping, like she was going down the biggest drop on the roller coaster, arms raised high in the air. But this time it wasn't fun. There was no end to the ride and nothing she could do to make it stop.

Danny was sitting on the top step, legs folded Indian style, with a big smile on his face.

"Danny, get out of my way," she said wearily.

"Make a tunnel, Kat." He was bobbing up and down. "Make a tunnel for me. Please, please, please." He liked to make his body rigid, like a surfboard, and slide down the steps through her legs.

"No. Just move."

Danny wiggled toward the wall. He was wearing his fuzzy blue Winnie-the-Pooh pajamas. "Are you going into your room now?"

"No, I'm going to climb up on the roof and get dressed in front of all the neighbors."

Danny cocked his head and looked at her strangely.

"Of course I'm going into my room, silly. Now get out of my way."

"Good." Danny did his countdown and slid down the steps, his head bumping along in the rear. That's probably why his brains are so scrambled, she thought.

When she went into her room there were five baseball cards lined up in a straight row on her pillow. Kat smiled and vowed to be nicer to her brother, at least for the rest of the day.

When she went downstairs, Danny was slurping Cheerios in the kitchen and her father had moved to the living room and was sitting on the couch, a stack of reports piled beside him and another cup of coffee in his hands. "Mrs. Darcy just called."

"She did?" Kat asked anxiously. "What did she say?"

"Well, it looks like Maggie is coming home today."

"Already? You mean she's all cured and everything? Is her leg all right? And what about that other thing that's wrong with her, is it okay? I can't believe this." Kat walked back and forth in front of the coffee table and jingled the change in her uniform pocket. She was glad that Maggie was coming home, but she did feel a certain twinge of panic. Maggie probably heard the news about the General's arrest, and Kat was sure that Maggie would find some connection between the accident and Kat's refusal to stop seeing the General. Maggie didn't think that anything happened just by chance. If Kat had only been able to get rid of Twitch before Maggie got back, she would at least have had that to offer as an olive branch.

Mr. O'Connor hesitated. "Kat, just calm down. Maggie wasn't magically cured overnight. She has to come home because of, well, it has something to do with her insurance coverage, that's all."

"You mean she doesn't have insurance, like, that lets her stay in the hospital?"

"Well, it seems that her dad hasn't quite kept up with his premium payments and there's not much money to pay the hospital bills. Mrs. Darcy will just take care of Maggie at home. When Mrs. Darcy's at work, Maggie's Aunt Gina will stay with her. Mrs. Olshefski has volunteered to help out, too."

"So, you mean that they're basically kicking her out because she doesn't have the money?"

"No. I didn't say that. The hospital would never discharge her if they thought that there was any danger to her health. It was a financial decision made by Mrs. Darcy, and maybe by Mr. Darcy too. I don't really know." Mr. O'Connor was biting on the end of his pen.

Maggie's father was both a dream and a nightmare. His

eyes, like Maggie's, were striking pale blue, but his hair was as thick as the night and as black as the sky when the moon was new. He was tall and he sang as he walked, no matter who was about casting him sidelong glances.

He didn't live with Maggie. Kat wasn't even sure if he lived in the same state. He didn't visit regularly but every once in a while he would just appear without warning. They would be walking home from school one day and there he would be, sitting on the front steps, humming and running his fingers through his hair, front to back, his head cocked to the side. Maggie would run to him, dropping her books anywhere, in the street, on the lawn, and he would fling her in the air. For the few days that he was around, all the other kids would envy Maggie. Mr. Darcy would take her out of school to go to the Mercer movies on Frankford Avenue in the middle of the week. They ate out every night and would spend long afternoons in Tiffany's Ice-Cream Parlor across from the arcade. Maggie thought that he was perfect. And then one day, he would be gone. Just like that. And sometimes he didn't come back for a whole year.

"So, she'll be okay?" Kat asked.

"Yes, she'll be okay. Dr. Madison will walk over and look in on her from time to time."

Dr. Madison was the pediatrician that all the kids had been going to since they were born. He worked out of an office that was in the basement of his house, on the corner of Guilford Street, just three blocks away. They all loved him. Sometimes it was worth getting sick just for the pleasure of visiting his office.

Mr. O'Connor picked up one of the fat reports from the couch. "Mrs. Darcy wants to know if you want to go over after school and spend the night with Maggie."

"Sure, I'll go over," Kat said.

"Okay, I already told her you probably would. Now you better get going. We'll talk about this later, all right?"

Kat went to the closet to get her coat. Her father looked up from his work. "Oh, by the way, did you know that they arrested Maggie's hit-and-run driver last night?"

"Yeah, I saw it on the news," she answered casually, avoiding his eyes. Kat pushed her arms into her jacket and quickly grabbed her book bag from the closet.

"Wasn't it that pigeon man that I told you to stay away from?"

"I guess so," she said and headed for the door. "I gotta go." She ran outside, but there was no escape. Out of the frying pan and into the fire, she thought.

Paul was waiting on the corner with a giant grin on his face.

Chapter
21

LAST NIGHT'S STORM was in evidence everywhere. The trees and bushes were shaking off cold wet drops with every gust of air, small rivers of water were running down the gutters beside the curbs picking up twigs, dead leaves, and old candy wrappers, and washing them all with a gurgle into the open mouth of the sewer. Bits of oil that had leaked from cars made dark swirling rainbows on the blacktop street. The sky looked like a lumpy gray comforter hung to dry, stretched end to end, and big fat drops were falling randomly from it. One hit Kat smack in the forehead and dribbled down her nose. She wiped it off with the back of her hand and tried to ignore Paul's good mood.

"So, did you hear the news?" Paul asked gleefully.

"Yeah, I heard and I don't want to talk about it."

"Can you believe it! The pigeon man runs Maggie over. He's always standing on that circle watching over all those filthy birds, but he doesn't care about slamming his car into Maggie. It could've even been me. It would've been me if Maggie didn't lose the toss. I bet he would've stopped if he hit a pigeon. Don't you think he would have stopped if he had hit a pigeon instead of a person? I hope they fry him."

"Paul!" Kat cried. "That's gross. Give me a break."

"Kat, don't tell me that you're still going to stick up for that guy after what he did. He's a major jerk. I thought for sure that you'd be ticked off at him."

"He probably didn't even know that he hit her, okay? It's not like he thinks normally like you and me. He had a tough life, okay?"

"Oh, the poor baby. I guess we ought to just let him get back in his car and run over a few more kids. Is that what you want? Admit it, Kat. You were wrong about him."

"Just forget it, Paul," Kat yelled. "You just don't understand. I said I didn't want to talk about it." She pulled her hood up over her head and kicked at a stone on the sidewalk.

"I can't believe you, Kat." Paul thrust his hands into his pockets and quickened his pace.

They walked in silence the rest of the way to school. When they got within a block of the school yard, Paul ran ahead and went in without so much as a glance at her.

Helen Hogan was planted on the corner across from the school, patiently waiting for Kat. Kat tried to ignore her and quickly crossed the street. But Helen was hard to shake. She fell in step with Kat.

"Kat! Did you hear?" Helen asked. "It was the pigeon man who ran Maggie over! And you, visiting him every day. Isn't it weird? My dad says they should have locked that guy up a long time ago. Those kind of people just shouldn't be—"

"Shut up, Helen."

"What?"

Kat stopped walking. She turned around and looked Helen in the face. "Just shut up, okay?"

"What's with you?" Helen asked, without even a pause.

Kat walked away without answering. She should have known better. Helen would never shut up, not as long as her heart was beating and there was still an ounce of breath left in her body.

"Well, fine. Be that way," Helen said, her voice rising. "But I'll tell you what, Kat O'Connor, you were wrong about that pigeon man. We all told you he would cause some kind of trouble. And the least you could do, for Maggie's sake, is admit it. What kind of friend are you, anyway?"

"You don't know what you're talking about," Kat snapped, turning around. "You don't know anything."

"Oh, really? I know how stupid you were going near that guy. Everybody thinks so. Even Maggie and Fran thought you were being weird."

Kat stopped in front of the school. She felt a blackness rising from the pit of her stomach. Everyone had apparently tried and convicted the General without any of the evidence. They had the noose around his neck and they were just waiting for Kat to kick the chair out from under him. She glared at Helen. "You're the stupid one, Helen. All of you are. And you're acting like a bunch of jerks. You don't know anything about the General. Why don't you try to find out a little bit about his side of the story."

"I know everything I need to know," Helen said, folding her arms across her chest. "I know that he hit Maggie and I know that you're still taking his side."

Fran had come up and was listening to the conversation. "C'mon, Kat. You can't deny it now," Fran added. "Think of what he did to Maggie."

"He didn't do it on purpose, Fran," Kat insisted.

"Oh, did you talk to him about it?" Helen sneered.

"No, but . . ."

"He . . . hit . . . Maggie. Then . . . he . . . drove . . . away," Helen said slowly, emphasizing each word as though Kat were an idiot. "It's not too complicated, Kat. At least not for those of us who aren't in love with him."

Kat's fists were clenched and she had a strong desire to stick one of them right in Helen's pinched little face. "You're brilliant, Helen. Just brilliant. You've got the whole thing figured out. So why don't you just get lost and leave me alone."

"Gladly!" Helen sniffed, turning away. "C'mon, Fran."

"But, Kat. . . ." Fran began.

"Just forget it, Fran," Kat sighed. "Just leave me alone."

Helen and Fran headed for the school yard, glancing back once at Kat and shaking their heads. She couldn't follow them. The school yard would be like a hornets' nest, stirred up by the news of the General's arrest, and Kat already felt stung and exposed. She went to stand behind the dripping Blessed Mother on the front lawn. It was quiet here and peaceful. No one could see her. Even with the bowing trees weeping on her and the cold soaking through her jacket as she leaned against the wet marble statue, she would prefer to stay here all day as to go into the warm classroom and face the "I told you so's" from the rest of the kids.

She watched the drops of rain as they slowly rolled from leaf to leaf, joining with other drops and picking up speed, until they became too heavy to cling to the tree any longer and fell, splattering to the concrete below. When the bell rang, she dragged herself into the school yard and slipped in quietly at the end of the line. But it did her no good.

"You're just in time for roll call, Lieutenant O'Connor," sniped Tyler Reid.

"Get a life, Tyler," Kat shot back.

"I've got a life, O'Connor. Not like someone we know who has to hang out with a dirtball pigeon man who runs over kids in his spare time."

The whole front half of the line snickered.

"I bet she was in on it from the beginning," Pete Castor said as the class was going up the stairs. "Trying to rub Maggie out, weren't you, Kat?"

"Shut up, Castor," Kat said angrily.

"Yeah, Castor. We can't talk because we don't know anything," Tyler sneered. "Kat says we're all just a bunch of dumb jerks."

Kat looked up at Helen. Helen narrowed her eyes at Kat, then flashed a small triumphant smile before heading into the hallway. Fran looked down at her feet. As she was coming in the classroom door, Kat got hit in the head with a spit ball.

"Maybe we could turn Kat in to the cops and get a reward or something," Justin said to a chorus of chuckles.

Kat's eyes searched desperately for Paul, but he had his back to her and he never turned around. She didn't know if she could bear the pain in her chest. She threw her coat in the closet and stumbled to her seat. She opened her history text and pretended to be absorbed in the words that were swimming before her eyes.

The door squeaked open and Sister Mildred clumped her way into the classroom.

"Silence!" she barked, and she scowled at them all.

For once, her formidable presence was not enough to entirely calm the class.

"Sister, Sister," Eric Polinski called out. "Did you know that they got the guy who ran over Maggie?"

"Yes, I heard." Sister Mildred eased herself into the chair behind her desk.

"Do you think he'll get the death penalty, Sister?" asked Tyler.

The nun crossed her arms and leaned forward on her desk, staring at the children. "That's highly unlikely, Mr. Reid. Mr. Ellison did not commit a capital offense."

The class moaned its disappointment. Kat was disgusted. Why didn't Sister Mildred tell them the General's story? He wasn't like a regular criminal. Maybe then they would all get off her back.

"I think he oughta fry," offered Chris Hutchinson.

"No, somebody ought to run him over with a car, just like he did to poor Maggie," suggested Dana Marzano.

Sister Mildred looked across the room as the students all offered their suggestions on how to properly punish the

General and she caught Kat's eye. It was a look of sadness and resignation and Kat knew that she was right. No matter what she or anybody else said, they hadn't known the General and they cared nothing for him. They would never understand. They didn't want to understand. The General was doomed.

"All right, enough." The nun cut into the class discussion. "I have news from Mrs. Darcy that Maggie will be coming home from the hospital today. I think we should all make her some cards wishing her well and Kathryn O'Connor can take them to her this afternoon."

"Yeah, great idea. That'll be like sending Benedict Arnold to comfort George Washington," someone hissed across the room.

Kat didn't even bother to look around to see who had said it. She was worried that Maggie was going to feel the same way.

"That will be quite enough!" the nun said sharply. "Now pass up the spelling punishment from last night. Anyone who did not complete the assignment will stand in the back of the room."

Kat bit her lip in dismay. Her face was flushed. She had completely forgotten about that stupid punishment. She cursed Tyler Reid under her breath, slowly rose and walked to the back of the room. She was the only one. Everyone turned and stared at her.

Sister Mildred glanced up from her desk and spied Kat. She folded her hands together and brought them up to her lips, thoughtfully, as though she were considering what sentence to pass. "Kathryn, why didn't you complete the assignment?"

"Well, I . . . something happened and . . . well, you know why I didn't do it," Kat said angrily. She didn't feel like discussing this in public.

"No, I don't know why," the nun snapped back. "I had lesson plans to complete last night, young lady, and I did them."

Kat's mouth opened to respond, but there was nothing she could say that wouldn't just get her in worse trouble. What were spelling chapters compared to the General's arrest and the trouble that it had gotten her into? She couldn't understand how Sister Mildred could work on lesson plans at that organized little desk while the General sat in jail, sick and terrified. So she just stood there for a minute with her mouth open and then clenched it shut and stared back at the nun in disbelief.

"Kathryn," the nun sighed. "The world does not stop for tragedy."

Kat shifted uncomfortably. She was beginning to feel a certain sympathy for Benedict Arnold. Maybe he was misunderstood.

Sister Mildred sighed again. "Just take your seat, Kathryn."

Kat couldn't concentrate on anything after that, but the nun kindly left her alone.

At recess all the other kids headed outside and the classroom was still and quiet. Kat crossed her arms on her desk and put her head down, thankful to be alone. She winced every time she thought about Paul. It was so hard to be in the same room with him and have him ignore her as if she meant nothing to him.

And some of the other kids were acting as if she had run Maggie over herself. She wished that she could do what they wanted, blame the General for the whole thing and hate him like everyone else did. She even tried, but it wouldn't work. He was just too gentle and hopeless.

She closed her eyes and dreamed that she was on the bed with the clean laundry. Relief flooded her body. Her mother was there, folding, smoothing, listening. She had never left! Kat reached to embrace her but something hit her in the back of the head. It was Tyler's ruler. Kat bolted up in her seat. The whole class had filed back in from recess and she hadn't heard them. She could feel her face burning but she glared at Tyler and stuck his ruler in her desk.

If the other kids thought she was acting like a jerk for not turning against the General, what was Maggie going to think? Maggie, who had begged her time after time to stay away from the General, who had warned her over and over that he was dangerous. Kat rested her head on her hand and thought of how she could explain the General to Maggie. Kat started three different letters to her friend, but scratched each one out with a deep, black X that bled through into the next page. It just wasn't working. The convincing words, the beautiful phrases, the poetry that used to dance in her head and leap onto the paper all lay wounded and flat. She couldn't make them rise. Everything she wrote, her journal, her school assignments, and even this letter to Maggie came out as dull and lifeless as a dictionary entry. She would never get Maggie to understand or forgive the General.

Kat thought of her friend stuck in a hospital bed, her leg hanging from a bar, not even able to reach a tissue to wipe away the tears that flowed down her face. Maggie had been convinced two days ago that the police would never find the driver of the car that had hit her and that Twitch had orchestrated the whole catastrophe. She couldn't condemn the General, even for Maggie, but Kat wanted desperately to do something to make her friend feel better and to smooth out any differences that there might be between them.

While the rest of the class worked on percentage problems, Kat wrote "DITCH TWITCH" at the top of her page and used Tyler's ruler to underline it. She began to work out a plan for getting rid of Twitch. That way, at least she would have something to offer Maggie this afternoon.

Chapter

22

KAT STOOD OUTSIDE Maggie's front door in the drizzle, her overnight bag hanging loosely in her hand. She looked down at the old worn welcome mat that sat on the landing before the front step. The heat of summer, the ice of winter, the children, the mailman, the raffle sellers and relatives, the parish priest, the ward leaders, the neighbors and friends, all had taken their toll, so that now, all that remained were half of the "M" and the final "E." The outer door was gray aluminum and the top half of it was screened. The screen was pulling away from the door in the upper left-hand corner and it hung down, a jagged triangle, and flapped with the breeze.

Kat practically lived here. She knew this house almost as well as her own. All the summers of her childhood she had flown in and out of this door dozens of times each day, never bothering to knock or to ring the bell. She freely raided the refrigerator for drinks and she knew where the cookies were kept and which drawers held the paint, the paper and the pencils. She never asked permission before pushing the coffee table out of the way so she could stretch out on the floor on her stomach and watch television or before descending into the dank, musty basement to poke around for the board games that were stored down there.

Maggie was a bit smaller than she was, but Kat still had free reign of the closet, and they shared clothes and cheap jewelry along with all the great secrets of their lives. It was here that she had retreated after her mother died. It was too painful to be in her own house. Every drawer she opened, every dish she used, every place she looked held some fresh wound. It was like poking about the ruins of a house after a tornado had passed through and sucked out every bit of air and life and precious memory.

And she couldn't show even half of what she felt with her father around. He was always watching her and worrying about how she was doing. Whenever he suggested that they talk about "things," she would bolt out of the room with some excuse. It wasn't that she didn't want to talk to him about her mother's death, she just couldn't. Whenever the subject came up between them, she would feel herself losing control. It was like when she was younger and would fall off her bike and get a gash in her knee. She could walk all the way home, stone-faced, pushing her bicycle and gritting her teeth at the pain in her leg. But the minute she walked into the house and saw the concern on her father's face, all her bravado would melt away and she would break down and cry. She avoided talking to her dad because she knew she would just lose it. She held her grief close, kept it quiet, and carried it like a rock in her heart.

At Maggie's though, she could say and do what she wanted. She could even unload some of her more selfish feelings, like how she hated having to do the laundry and matching all of Danny's little socks, and how they never got to eat a decent meal unless Mrs. Darcy or Mrs. Olshefski sent one over. Maggie just listened and nodded her head thoughtfully and brought out magazines and games to take her mind off it all.

She had never noticed the rust around the door handle before or how the cement step was cracked and pulling away from the house. Kat shifted her bag from hand to hand and zipped it open to check once again if she had forgotten anything. She bent down to retie her shoes.

The door swung open. "Hello, Kat." Mrs. Darcy smiled down at her through the opening in the screen. "I thought I saw someone standing by the door. I didn't hear you knock. Come on in. Maggie's been waiting for you."

The living room was transformed. The coffee table was beside the television at the bottom of the stairs and Maggie was lying in a big hospital-type bed that was smack in the middle of the room. The end table by the couch was littered with soda cans, medicine bottles, and a few sticky spoons.

The girls stared at each other for a few awkward moments.

"I'll be upstairs. Call if you need anything." Mrs. Darcy

retreated to the spare bedroom she used for sewing. They soon heard the hum of her machine.

Kat stood by the wall, a few steps from where she had come in. "So, how you feeling?"

"Okay, I guess," Maggie answered. She was watching the blank television.

"I got some cards here for you. Turtle made everybody make one." Kat unzipped her bag.

"You gotta be kidding," Maggie said, and turned to watch Kat take the drawings out.

"No, really."

"This ought to be a howl. What does she think I am, a first-grader or something?" Maggie started to flip through the cards and Kat returned to her position against the wall, still holding onto her bag.

"Kat, you can sit down, you know."

"You sure you want me to?"

Maggie dropped the homemade cards on her lap. "Listen, Kat. I'll admit, I was really mad when I heard that it was the pigeon man who ran me over. I mean, I told you he was weird. And then, you got cursed by Twitch and wouldn't listen to me and everything got all fouled up." Maggie was trying to scratch the back of her hand up under her cast.

Kat turned dejectedly toward the door. "Okay, I'll just go. I figured that it wasn't your idea to invite me over here today, anyway."

"No. Wait a minute. Don't go. It was my idea to have you over. I mean, the more I thought about it, the more I

134

realized that it wasn't really your fault. It wasn't even the pigeon man's fault. You two were just mediums."

"We were what?"

"Mediums. You know, Twitch just went through you to get me. If it wasn't you, it would've been somebody else. She just used you. She can do whatever she wants. Even if you hadn't ever talked to that stupid pigeon man, I'd still be lying here all messed up."

"Oh." Kat stood silently trying to figure out if Maggie was letting her off the hook. It was sometimes hard to follow Maggie's train of thought.

"Besides, I can't really be mad at you."

"You can't?"

"No. Well, realistically, let's look at my options here. If I ditch you as my best friend, who am I going to hook up with?" Maggie grabbed one of the cards out of the pile on her lap. "Yeah, here's one. Lisa Adamcyk. A girl who can talk for a solid hour about fingernail colors and cuticles. Give me a break. Or how about this one, Beth Gilmore, whose goal in life is to own a corner row house and raise ten kids and vacuum the stairs every other day. Gag me."

Kat flopped into a chair and smiled fondly at Maggie. "They're not all that bad. What about Fran and Jennifer and Kelly?"

"Well, okay, they're not all bimbos, but there isn't anybody like you. I'm getting out of this stupid neighborhood as soon as I'm old enough, and you're coming with me. We'll go to Paris and London and everywhere and you'll write great books and I'll, well, I'll do something important.

Maybe I'll be your agent. God, I wish I were older." Maggie looked down at her legs. "Actually, right now I'd be happy if I could just stand up."

"How's the leg?" Kat asked.

"It itches like crazy, but it doesn't hurt. They're going to x-ray it in five weeks and then decide what to do." Maggie sat silently for a few moments staring at her leg.

"You okay?" Kat asked.

"Yeah. I'm okay," Maggie said, straightening up. "It's just that I don't want to have an operation if it's not going to fix everything, you know? I mean, if they're not sure, what's the point? I don't like that whole anesthesia thing. Sometimes people don't wake up from that."

"Oh, Maggie. I'm so sorry that this whole thing happened," Kat said. "But I just have this feeling that you're going to be okay. I'm sure it's all going to work out."

"Not as long as I'm stuck in this place," Maggie said, "with el creepo next door."

"Twitch?"

"Of course Twitch. I mean, Hooperman's a creep too, but I can handle him. At least he yells at you right to your face. But Twitch, I just can't take her anymore. I'm sick of her staring out her window spying on me all the time, watching everything I do."

"Yeah, me too," Kat sympathized.

"But at least you don't live right next door. You've got sweet Mrs. Olshefski next to you, babysitting and baking cookies. I've got the escapee from hell. I think that she listens to me through the walls at night, too."

"How?" Kat asked.

"I don't know, but she does. From Hooperman's side we hear the television all the time. We hear his dog barking. We hear Mrs. Hooperman's stereo. You know what we hear from Twitch's wall? Nothing. Absolutely nothing. It's just not normal. Frankly, it's driving me crazy. I read this book once, and it was a true story, about this kid who had a really weird neighbor. He tried to warn everybody but nobody would listen. One day they found the kid dead on the neighbor's back porch."

"Maggie, are you serious?" Kat asked. "That really happened?"

"Yeah. I just know that someday they'll find me dead with a black knife sticking out of my chest. Promise me that if I'm ever missing you'll make the police search Twitch's house."

"I promise, Maggie, but—"

"I'm telling you, Kat, I just can't stand it anymore. I just wish we could move. I mean, look at me now," Maggie said, eyes wide. "I couldn't even run away if she tried anything."

Kat remembered the plan she had worked on during math. "Maggie, maybe instead of you getting out, we can get Twitch to move."

"Yeah, right. And maybe we can get the Pope to move the Vatican next door."

Kat rustled around in her bag. "No, really. I mean it. I've been working on this plan to get rid of her while you were in the hospital. I think it could work. We could even start on it tonight. Here." Kat handed the paper to Maggie.

"Ditch Twitch?"

"Ditch Twitch." Kat smiled.

Chapter
23

Mrs. Darcy had made her famous spaghetti for dinner. It was Maggie's favorite. Kat sat crosslegged on the floor with her plate in her lap, and Maggie ate off of a special tray that fit across her bed. Mrs. Darcy was her usual silent self and took her meal alone in the kitchen.

"Aren't some of the things you've got here illegal?" Maggie asked, twirling the pasta around her fork and tapping at the plan with her spoon.

"Like what?" Kat asked.

"Well, for instance, I think it's against the law to burn down people's shrubbery. Anyway, it's such an overgrown mess that it would be like a regular forest fire. And what if my house catches fire? I mean, I do live right next door, you know."

"Okay," Kat said, "so we don't burn down any bushes.

We could start with the threatening letters. You know, move out of this neighborhood or else sort of stuff. And then we could give her warnings. Like the first week she's still around after we tell her to move, we could put garbage on her front step. If she's still there the next week, we send another letter and break a window or two. Each week we make it worse until she's sick of it and moves away."

Maggie took a gulp of milk and wiped her mouth on the sleeve of her robe. "Kat, you're so naive."

"What are you talking about, naive? I am not."

"Who do you think we're dealing with here, Mrs. Hooperman? Kat, this is Twitch. Those things aren't going to bother her. And even if they did, don't you think she'd make us pay?"

"That's what Paul said," Kat mumbled to her plate.

"Paul? You mean you told him about this?"

"Well, I mentioned it."

"Let me guess," Maggie laughed. "He's thinking it over."

"Yeah. He's thinking it over. Let's just leave him out of this." Kat winced at the mention of Paul's name. For the first time she could ever remember he had avoided her all day. She had never felt so lonely at school as she had today. "Well, I'm sorry that you think my plan is so stupid. I guess you'd prefer to just sit around and get cursed the rest of your life," Kat snapped.

"No, stupid. We've just got to fight fire with fire."

"Which means?"

"Which means we have a séance. You know, the kind of

thing they use to rid places of evil spirits. I can't believe I didn't think of it before. I saw it in an old *Reader's Digest* article when I was in the hospital."

"So you think you know how to do one of these séances?" Kat stood up and put her plate on the coffee table.

"You don't *do* séances, Kat. You *conduct* them. And yes, I think I would be great at it. See if you can find the *Reader's Digest*. My mom unpacked my stuff upstairs. It's probably on the nightstand beside my bed."

Kat ran up the steps to Maggie's room and found the magazine. On the cover there was a drawing of a young girl in rain gear standing beside a flood swollen river and the headline, "Heroism in Heart Creek Canyon." Kat ran her finger down the table of contents to the entry "Serious About Séances." The article was on page 113. She flipped it open and read the bold faced words boxed and highlighted on each page and the captions under the pictures. There were drawings of devils and other ghouls and a shot of a very large woman in a flowered gown wearing lots of jewelry. She brought the magazine down to Maggie.

"I'm not sure about this, Maggie. It kind of gives me the creeps."

"Yeah, well, Twitch gives me the creeps, too. And if a séance can get rid of her, it'll be worth it." Maggie grabbed the remote control and turned on the television. "You read the story and then we'll plan what we're going to do. We'll wait till my mom goes to bed."

Kat curled up in the armchair in the corner of the room and began to read about a woman from El Paso who raised spirits from the dead so that their loved ones could converse with them once again and who exorcised evil demons from haunted houses. Kat didn't believe that people's spirits could come back from the dead. She had yearned and ached for her mother so much these past few months. How many hours had she spent lying in bed crying and remembering and reaching out with her whole soul in the darkness for just a touch of what she had lost. There was nothing. If ever two spirits could connect across that great chasm between life and death, it was Kat and her mother.

But she wasn't so sure that evil demons didn't really exist. She read on about houses where books flew off of shelves and statues cried tears of blood. People were thrown up against walls and some knocked unconscious by invisible forces when they tried to interfere with demons.

"Maggie, I don't think we ought to do this." Kat closed the magazine without finishing the article. "I don't like it."

"Why? What's the matter?" Maggie pressed the mute button on the remote control. She was watching a rerun of "Gilligan's Island."

"It's too creepy. I hate this stuff."

"You mean you're just afraid," Maggie sniffed.

"Well what if Twitch gets really ticked off and does one of the things they talk about in this magazine?"

"Kat, I've already been hit by a car, knocked unconscious, and had my leg screwed up for the rest of my life. What else could she do to me?" Maggie lowered her voice. "And now she's messing around with my head too, and I've got to do something to stop it."

"What do you mean?"

"I just can't stand going to sleep, Kat," Maggie said,

struggling to keep her voice even. "I have these nightmares. Weird nightmares. Every time I close my eyes. You don't know what it's like to wake up in the middle of the night, all sweaty with your heart pounding a mile a minute, and scared out of your mind."

Kat knew, but she said nothing.

"I know it's really stupid," Maggie said slowly, staring at her hands. "But the whole thing is making me afraid of . . . well maybe not afraid . . . but kind of just a little worried about . . . cars. I just couldn't stop shaking when they were bringing me home today. The ambulance guys didn't have a clue. They kept piling blankets on me." Maggie looked up at Kat. "It's not really that dumb if you think about it. There's nothing between you and the other car except a skinny yellow line. Just one little flick of somebody's wrist and boom, you're done for. I guess I just never thought about it before the accident, you know?"

"But, Maggie . . ."

"Swear you won't tell anybody," Maggie interrupted.

"Maggie, you know I would never tell and besides, I don't think it's weird at all."

"Swear you won't tell Paul."

That won't be a problem, Kat thought sadly. "I swear."

"Well, anyway," Maggie said, "I'm going to fight back against Twitch either with or without you." Maggie turned the sound back on the television. The Skipper was slapping Gilligan on the head with his cap as their latest hope for rescue disappeared out of the lagoon and headed for the horizon.

Kat sighed and reopened the magazine. She was reading about weeping walls and floating furniture when suddenly there was a large crash and a scream. Kat jumped from her chair and turned toward the door, her heart beating rapidly and her fingertips tingling. The doorbell rang.

"Can you get that, Kat?" Mrs. Darcy called from the kitchen. She was washing the dishes in the sink.

Kat opened the door slowly. "Dad!"

"Sorry," Mr. O'Connor said. "Danny tripped up the step and fell into the door."

Kat was about to tell Danny what a doofus he was—he never watched where he was going—but stopped herself when she saw that he was stealthily wiping away his tears and trying to look brave and unaffected.

"Do I have to come home or something?" Kat asked.

"No," her father said through the screen. "But I just got a call that I have to be down at the printer's right away. There's some sort of problem with the manual I just submitted. You've got to keep Danny with you for a while."

"But, Dad," Kat moaned. "Can't he go with you or something? I don't want to have him annoying us all night."

"I'm sorry, Kat, there's just no other way. Mrs. Olshefski's away visiting her sister and it's too late to get a babysitter. I wouldn't ask you if it wasn't important. If I'm not back by eight-thirty, you'll have to bring him home and put him to bed."

Mrs. Darcy appeared at the door. "Danny's welcome to sleep over with the girls if he wants to."

"Hello, Grace," Mr. O'Connor said. "I don't want to

impose on you. Kat can just bring him home. I'm hoping I won't be out too late."

"It's not an imposition. He's welcome to stay. Do you want to stay here tonight with the big girls, Danny?" Mrs. Darcy asked.

Danny was smiling and biting his lower lip. "I guess so," he answered.

"You're sure about this, Grace?" Mr. O'Connor asked.

"Yes, it's no problem at all. Danny's a good boy."

"Okay, then, I'll just run home and get his things. Kat will watch out for him and get him off to bed and all. I really appreciate this."

Mr. O'Connor leaned down and scooped Danny up in his arms. "Okay, big guy, you be real good. Do you understand? You do whatever Kat says. Promise?"

"Promise!" Danny said, his hand pressed to his forehead in a military salute.

"Give me a big hug because I might not be home in time to tuck you in."

Danny wrapped his arms around his father's neck and gave a long hard squeeze. Kat stood, watching them through the screen, her hand holding the cold damp doorknob.

"See ya later, alligator." Danny slipped down off his father and ran in to Maggie.

"Thanks, Kat. I'd be lost without you." Mr. O'Connor gave her a smile through the screen and turned and left. Kat stood by the door for a few minutes and hugged her arms to her body.

Her night was ruined. Instead of spending the night just crashing and hanging out with Maggie she'd have to follow Danny around and make sure he didn't destroy anything of Mrs. Darcy's. He'd be pestering her for juice every five minutes and whining for candy and treats. He'd be poking his nose into whatever she and Maggie did and complaining that he was bored and begging for his videos.

Maggie didn't seem to mind. Danny was up on her bed and she was showing him how to push the buttons to make it go up and down.

"Look, Kat," he squealed. "It's a ride. I'm doing it myself. Wanna see?"

Maggie motioned Kat closer and whispered in her ear. "Don't worry. We'll do the séance at midnight. It's the best time, anyway."

Kat looked at her watch. It was six-thirty. In five and a half hours, she would be participating in her first séance.

Chapter

24

KAT LAY PERFECTLY STILL in the darkness and listened to the faint ticking of the mantel clock. The streetlight on the telephone pole outside sent a weak yellow glow through the front windows of the house, just enough to give the dark objects in the room a dim shadowy outline. She heard an occasional car in the distance and the regular hum of the refrigerator. Otherwise, all was silent.

She was on the couch wrapped in an afghan, still dressed, her sneakers untied but hanging loosely on her feet. She had tried to close her eyes several times, but they seemed to just pop open again of their own accord. Her mind was racing through all the events of the day and sleep was impossible. And so she lay there and traced all the black objects in the room with her eyes, verifying the bookcase and the coatrack and feeling some momentary attacks of panic when there was something she couldn't identify right away. It was raining again. She could hear the drops slapping against the window and there was a low rumble of thunder in the distance.

The hands of the clock were moving toward midnight. Kat listened to Maggie's regular breathing and decided not to wake her. Kat felt that she was no match for witches and demons, and she would much rather break a few windows in daylight than hold a séance in the dead of a stormy night. She closed her eyes and rubbed her temples, trying to relax enough for sleep. It had been a frustrating night. It took her over an hour and a half to get Danny to sleep. He had had six glasses of water, three crying fits, and four trips to the bathroom. He seemed frightened to be away from home. Twice he had screamed out for his mother instead of her and when she went up and saw him sitting in the middle of Maggie's big bed, clutching at the covers, she realized that he missed his mother, in his own way, a lot more than she had realized.

After Mrs. Darcy had gone to bed, she and Maggie talked, in their usual way, about friends and fears and family problems until each fell silent and kept company with her own thoughts. Kat thought about telling Maggie the General's story, but decided against it. At the very mention of the General's name, Maggie's eyes narrowed and her jaw clenched. She hated him and Kat could not blame her. Maggie would never see the General as a gentle, confused old man, but always as the heartless villain who crushed her leg and haunted all her dreams.

Sometimes, Kat felt like she was the only sighted person in a blind world. People just didn't care and rushed on with their stupid lives no matter what happened. The death of her mother was no more to them than the squashing of a bug on a busy street. They didn't stop. They didn't hurt. They didn't even notice. Her life was ruined. She knew that she would never be happy again. But what did it mean to them? Nothing.

"Kat! Are you awake?" Maggie called quietly.

Kat lay perfectly still and feigned sleep. She definitely didn't have the heart to grapple with spirits tonight.

"Kat. Kat, wake up!" Maggie whispered, a bit louder this time.

Kat heard a flapping noise and felt a sharp jab in her forehead. "Ouch!" She jumped up and the afghan fell to the floor. Maggie had thrown the *Reader's Digest* at her.

"Sorry, but I had to wake you up. It's almost midnight. You okay? I didn't mean to hit you in the head." Maggie had risen up on her elbows to almost a sitting position. She looked ghostly, like a mournful apparition, her pale skin and white nightgown standing out eerily from the darkness all around her. "It's time," she said in a low voice.

Maggie motioned Kat closer with her hand. "You're going to have to get the stuff we need, but be real quiet. We can't afford to wake up my mom. There's a fat candle on the shelf in the cellar way and the matches are behind the clock. Get a saucer from the kitchen too, so that we don't drip wax all over my bed."

Kat went reluctantly to get the materials. The

floorboards creaked under her weight, something she had never noticed during the day. The door to the basement was in the dining room. She hated basements at night. The door squealed as she opened it and she hesitated.

"Go on, go on," the ghostlike Maggie hissed. Her glowing arm was outstretched and she was pointing insistently at the door, like the ghost of Christmas past before the vision of Scrooge's tombstone. "It's just on the right, on the shelf."

Kat stood on the landing. She couldn't see anything. The musty smell of the basement rose up to her and filled her with dread. It was like standing at the mouth of a dank hole, a yawning grave at the center of the earth. All her fears were just below, in the blackness of a basement.

She felt around with her foot for the top step and sat on it. She ran her hand along the right wall until she felt the low shelf. On the end, just as Maggie had said, was the candle. She grabbed it and quickly closed the squeaky door behind her, feeling her way back through the dining room with enormous relief.

Maggie lit the match and then the candle and they left a faint smell of smoke in the air. Kat sat at the foot of the bed with Maggie propped up at its head, her injured leg still hanging bleakly from the metal bar above. The candle was between them. Its flame flickered gently and made the shadows dance against the walls.

"Okay, are you ready?" Maggie asked.

Kat nodded, but she wasn't telling the truth. Maggie couldn't get as close to the candle as she wanted because of how she was tethered to the bed. She bent her head forward.

Her face was draped in the shadows, but the orange light reflected in her eyes. "Let's join hands," she said in a low voice full of determination. "Now, close your eyes and concentrate really hard. Think about pushing Twitch away with the sheer power of your mind. Think about breaking her spirit into thousands of pieces and scattering it into the wind. I'll do the chanting. Some of it may be in tongues. Don't worry. I'm going to say whatever the spirits put into my mouth. If something happens to me, you'll have to take over. Don't stop. That's just what she would want. We have to be really strong to fight her."

"Maggie," Kat whispered desperately. "I don't know if I can do this." The darkness was pressing in all around her and she felt very weak.

"You have to. You have to," Maggie said between clenched teeth. "You can do it. Just be strong." She squeezed Kat's hands, her right one warm and firm, her casted left hand cool and weak. "Here we go."

Kat closed her eyes and Maggie began to chant. Kat felt as though the room were spinning and Maggie's sing-song voice was making it go. The candle was giving off a faint hot-sweet smell that was making her sick to her stomach. Her palms were all sweaty and she could feel the nails of Maggie's long bony fingers digging into her skin. She tried to concentrate on banishing Twitch, but it wasn't working. Kat began to feel that sensation of the cold snake again coiling up around her neck. She took a deep nervous breath. Then she heard it. It was unmistakable. Something was moving in the room. She opened her eyes. A shadow flew across the wall. Kat began to panic.

She pulled her hands away from Maggie's. She had to stop this thing. Suddenly, the front door swung open violently and crashed against the wall. The candle blew out, plunging them into darkness. There was a loud piercing scream outside. Kat jumped up and stood trembling beside the bed. Maggie stopped chanting. The screen door flapped in the wind and the rain was blowing into the house. Kat held her breath for several terrifying seconds. Then she heard the scream again, only this time it was farther away.

Kat turned toward Maggie. "Danny! That's Danny's scream. I know it."

"Oh, my God!" Maggie whispered. "Twitch has him. She took him instead of us!"

Kat ran up the stairs and checked Danny's bed. Her brother was gone. She raced back down the steps. "I'm going after him."

"Kat, wait!" Maggie called after her. "Don't do it. We'll get help."

"I'm going," Kat hollered. "There isn't time." And she ran out the door.

Chapter

25

A COLD RAIN WAS FALLING and it was windy and everything was shrouded in gloom. Danny was gone. Kat felt as though her heart were beating in her throat and she tried to swallow it back down. Twitch's front windows were dark. Kat ran down the steps and around the corner to the back of the house. There was a faint glow on the second floor from behind the edges of the drawn shades. Kat stealthily climbed the slippery iron stairs that led to Twitch's rear door. If unlocked, it should open into the kitchen just as in her own house. She crouched low and reached up to try the handle but it didn't turn. She held her ear to the door but there was no sound, only the insistent rain slapping against the peeling paint. She knew that she couldn't force it open. She held on to the metal arm rail and leaned over the hedge to check out the yard below.

There should have been a basement door down there somewhere, but with the darkness and the overgrown bushes, she couldn't see it.

Kat pushed her dripping hair out of her eyes. She could see a square of light coming from the second floor, a window without a shade. There was a small ledge of about six inches above the stonework that rimmed the first floor. Kat quickly tied her shoes and, sucking in her breath, gingerly eased herself off the metal balcony and onto the ledge. The rain lashed at her bare arms and the bricks that made up the second floor wall were cold and wet. The dying evergreen tree on the plot behind her was thrashing in the wind and the honeysuckle vines that entwined it seemed to be reaching out to capture her.

Kat pressed her body close against the brick and slowly inched her way around the corner to the side of the house, trying not to look down. Her fingertips gripped at the mortar between the bricks and her every move was precarious. She couldn't stop thinking about Danny—about the baseball cards from this morning and the little hugs he sometimes gave her, the books they had read while he sat on her lap and the way she had held him that first day he found out about their mother's death. She didn't care if she died trying, she was going to find him and get him safely home.

She was almost there. It was such slow going. Her legs ached from the strain of moving across the small ledge and her left cheek was scratched and bleeding from rubbing against the brick. She reached out with her right hand and caught the ledge of the window. She had better balance now and quickly pulled herself even with the window. The rain was making it hard for her to see anything clearly. With her hand she wiped away the dripping water and a whole layer of grime came off on her fingers. She pressed her face against the glass. She was trying to make out the figures within when there was a cry and something jumped at her from inside the house, scratching up against the glass. Kat screamed and threw herself backward, instinctively. Too late she saw it had been the cat. She clutched at the air for a few horrifying seconds and then fell, painfully crashing into a large azalea bush below.

Kat lay still for a few moments and the rain pelted her in the face. She groaned and tried to move. The branches were cutting her arms and catching in her clothes. She closed her eyes and wondered miserably if she had the strength to call for help. There was a noise. It was the muffled squeal of a door opening and a rustling beyond the hedge. Kat turned her head. To her horror she saw a dark shrouded figure moving slowly toward her. She opened her mouth to scream, but she was paralyzed with fear and all that came out was a low pitiful whine. The figure came closer and reached out its dripping arms, taking Kat's face in its cold hands. She couldn't breathe. It bent down over her. A gust of wind blew the hood off of its head. Kat felt as though her heart had stopped. There hanging over her was the most hideous face she had ever seen. It was Twitch. She raised her arms to fend the witch off, but she felt her life draining away and everything went black.

Chapter

26

"KAT. KAT." A SOFT VOICE was calling to her. Kat slowly came back from the darkness. The ache in her back and the cuts on her face and arms throbbed and made her sorely aware that she was still alive. She lifted her lids with great effort and her eyes struggled to focus. She was indoors. Someone was beside her pressing a cold washcloth to her forehead. She reached up and touched the hand. The skin was soft, squishy almost, and slipped around over the bones like a soapy dishrag. The lights were dim, but Kat finally began to make sense of the objects around her. She looked up and suddenly realized that the form beside her was Twitch in all her horridness. Kat let out a small cry and clutched at the cover that was tucked up around her neck.

"It's all right, Kathryn, dear," the witch said. Her voice was thin and shaky, but it had a sparkle to it, like the music of wind chimes touched gently by a June breeze.

Kat thrust the hand away from her forehead and shuddered. But Twitch hung over her still, staring ghoulishly, and Kat shrunk back against the couch. Her heart was racing. She knew that she should do something, but she felt like she was under a spell. Her mind was in a fog and her body was frozen. She studied the witch. She was old and hideous. The skin on the left side of her face was discolored and stretched taut so that her eyeball was exposed and seemed to stick out glaringly. She had no eyelashes or eyebrows, but a whole head full of long wild white hair. Her lips were drawn back from her mouth and you could see all of her large yellow teeth. It was as though her face were frozen in a disgusting sneer.

Twitch backed away from the couch slightly and pulled a dark shawl that hung on her shoulders up around the bottom half of her face. "I'll go make you a nice cup of tea to perk you up," she said. "Now you lie still and don't try to move a bit."

Kat watched the witch disappear into the kitchen and then quickly surveyed her situation. She was stretched out on a couch in a strange-looking room with low lights. It had to be the living room since all the houses on the block had the same layout. That would mean that the front door was about ten feet behind her. She had to find Danny and get out before Twitch came back. She struggled to a sitting position. There was a sharp pain in her back and her head was throbbing. "Danny!" Kat called in a hoarse whisper. There was no answer. He could be either upstairs or in the basement. The teakettle began to whistle. Kat got to her feet with great effort and started stiffly toward the basement door. She moved as fast as her ailing body could take her, but she was too late. Twitch grabbed her arm as she was reaching for the handle.

"Oh, no, dear. You have to lay down. I would feel terrible if you got yourself hurt. Now onto the couch. I have my orders, you know." Twitch led her to the couch and Kat reluctantly dropped back onto it. Injured as she was, she probably still could have pushed the old woman to the floor and made it into the basement. But she couldn't bring herself to do it. She wasn't sure why, but a speck of indecision had lodged in her brain and she needed to move more slowly until the thing worked its way out.

Kat wondered if she was being mesmerized. Though she was repulsed by the hideous face there was an irresistible force which kept drawing her back to it and she couldn't help staring into the odd eyes. There was something about them that held her.

She had expected that Twitch would be gruesome and she was. But it was somehow different than what she had thought. Kat had always imagined that the witch would have small darting eyes with a fierceness of spirit and a violence of soul. But this woman, hovering over her in a dark, cloaklike dress with a cup of boiling tea in her hand, didn't subdue Kat with a strong arm, but seemed to lull her into a groggy state of powerlessness.

"Take some tea, Kat," Twitch said in her musical voice, and held a teaspoonful up to Kat's lips.

"No, no," Kat said, turning her head. "I won't take it."

She wondered what was in the cup and whether Danny had been given the same thing.

"It's called lemon soother. It's an herbal tea," Twitch said, reading Kat's mind, stirring the concoction and clinking the spoon against the sides of the cup. "It always makes me feel better."

"No!" Kat said with finality.

"All right. All right," Twitch said and put the cup and saucer on the mantel next to a row of soft dolls. They wore gingham and print dresses with lace at the hems and their faces were embroidered in cloth. Kat noticed that dolls were sitting all over the room in various degrees of completion.

Twitch took the middle one off the mantel and returned to Kat's side. "I modeled this one after you," she said. "Do you like it?"

Kat nodded in wonder. The doll had her round features and the yarn that hung down its back in a tight braid was the exact brown of her own hair. The dress it wore was even similar to the one her mother had made for her confirmation in the sixth grade. She had heard of voodoo before, but none of these dolls had twisted limbs or protruding needles.

"I made it two years ago. Pretty, isn't it? I couldn't bring myself to give it away."

"You give them away?" Kat asked, her eyes taking in all the little faces peering out from the dimness.

"Many of them, yes. I do manage to sell quite a few at craft fairs."

"You go to craft fairs?" Kat said incredulously.

"No, no. I would like to, of course." She moved away

from the couch and lovingly rearranged the positions of the dolls on the mantel, smoothing their dresses and untangling their bangs as though they were real children who needed her attention. "But I don't move around too well." Twitch patted her left hip with her hand. "I hurt my hip years ago in a fall." She was retying the shoelaces of the last doll in the row. "And, of course, there's the light. It's rather uncomfortable for me."

Kat looked at the dim lamps and the heavy drapes with renewed trepidation. Maggie had often said that witches, vampires, and other creatures of the darkness could not bear the light. But they probably didn't make sweet-faced dolls either. Kat fingered the one in her hand and admired the detail, the faintly smiling mouth, the crisp stitched collar.

She watched Twitch move around the room, repositioning the dolls and wrapping up loose balls of yarn. It could be a trick, but so far Twitch didn't seem particularly evil or menacing. Kat felt that she was slowly losing her grip on the hatred she had held for so long against her neighbor.

"This doll is really neat," Kat ventured, searching Twitch's eyes. "You did a great job. I actually used to have a dress like this one."

"I know," Twitch answered. "I also know how you ruined it."

"You do?"

"Sure. I couldn't have missed that commotion even if I was half deaf."

"It wasn't my fault, though," Kat said, a small smile playing across her face at the memory.

"Of course not," Twitch chuckled.

"I wouldn't have had to climb the tree in the first place if Hooperman . . . I mean . . . Mr. Hooperman hadn't let Sheba out. I don't like Dobermans, and Sheba's so nasty."

"Sheba's got nothing on Hooperman. At least I have an excuse for my scary face. Here's my Hooperman impression." Twitch screwed up her scarred face into an angry scowl, but she couldn't hold it for long. She threw her head back and let out a high-pitched laugh that filled the room. It was infectious. Kat couldn't help but smile.

"And how about this," Twitch said. "I call this one 'the Hooperman stomp'." She paced back and forth before the couch, head lowered, feet clumping and arms pumping with militaristic fervor.

It was too much for Kat. The sight of this deformed old woman in a dark dress mimicking Mr. Hooperman broke her up.

"Don't make me laugh," Kat pleaded. "It hurts too much."

"Oh, my. I'm sorry," Twitch said, gently stroking Kat's arm. "Don't tell Dr. Madison about this. He gave me strict instructions to keep you quiet and comfortable."

"Dr. Madison was here?" Kat asked, surprised.

"Yes, of course. I called him after you fell into the yard." Twitch smiled. "I couldn't quite carry you up here myself, you know. He's with Danny right now."

"Danny!" Kat cried, bolting upright. She had almost forgotten him. "Then he was here!"

"Danny? No, why would Danny be here? He apparently

fell outside in the darkness running around looking for your father. I don't know the whole story. Dr. Madison carried you up to the couch here and was checking you out when your father came in and asked for help with Danny. It's been quite a night. I'm supposed to be watching over you until he gets back. How am I doing?"

"Good," Kat smiled. "You're a regular Clara Barton."

"All I need is the uniform. Do you think I could get you to drink some of that tea with me now?"

Kat looked at the deformed little woman. She couldn't believe it. Here she was, lying on the couch in Twitch's house late at night. And instead of being afraid or repulsed, she was actually starting to enjoy herself.

"Sure," Kat said. "I'd love some tea. Can I help you?"

"No, no," Twitch said. "Definitely not. Remember, I'm Clara Barton and I'm supposed to be taking care of you. I'm slow, but I'm efficient. You lie still, and I'll be right back."

Twitch limped her way into the kitchen to heat more water and Kat snuggled down into the couch. Even with her sore back and a throbbing head, she felt more relaxed and comfortable than she had in ages. It was like she was on a vacation from her real life and the flight home was delayed indefinitely.

Chapter 27

"CAREFUL, NOW. DON'T SPILL IT," Twitch said, handing Kat the hot cup of tea. "We don't want to add any burns to your list of injuries."

Twitch took some extra pillows and arranged them behind Kat's head. Kat winced a little with the change of position.

"Do you mind if I ask you what you were doing up on that ledge in the middle of the night?" Twitch asked. "Just out of curiosity. You're the first visitor I ever had who tried to come in through the window."

Kat felt her face turning bright red and she looked down into her cup. "Well, it's a long story. I'm really sorry. It's just that I couldn't find Danny and . . . and . . ."

"You thought I had stolen him."

"Well, sort of," Kat stammered. "I just didn't know where he was."

"No need to worry," Twitch said. "I limit myself to eating only one small child per week. I already had my fill on Tuesday."

"I'm so sorry," Kat said, wishing she could melt into the couch and disappear.

"It's okay," Twitch said. "I've done things a lot worse. A whole lot worse. Besides, I'm glad in a way. Otherwise we wouldn't have had this visit."

"Why don't you ever come outside?" Kat asked. "Is it because of us?"

"No, no," Twitch said. "It's too painful for me to get around and I have a sensitivity to the light. I just can't bear it anymore. I have everything I need here. I read and make my dolls. I like to watch the play and the bustle on the street. And my sister comes for visits."

"Your sister?" Kat sat up a little on the couch.

"Yes. You know, female relative of the same parentage. I didn't just crawl out from under a rock one day."

"I know. I didn't mean that. It's just that . . ." Kat laid her throbbing head back on the pillows.

"Why, she's even older than me. You should see the two of us. Takes us half the day just to get up from the kitchen table and make it into the living room." Twitch slapped her knee and laughed. "We grew up in this house together," she said, looking around the dim room. "Used to race all around this place. Don't tell her I said so," Twitch whispered, leaning toward Kat, "but I'm still faster."

Kat rubbed her forehead. Her mind was racing but the thoughts were jumbled up with the pain and she couldn't seem to focus on the picture that was trying to emerge.

"Here," Twitch said, pulling an almost-finished doll from beside her chair. "Who do you think that is?"

"It looks like Donna," Kat said, running her finger slowly across the freckled face and picturing the stuck-up girl who lived across the street. "How do you get the expressions so perfect? It's amazing."

Twitch winked, contorting the whole side of her face. "Well, I've been studying my subjects for years. All these dolls have personalities," she said, her arm sweeping the room. "It's more fun to work on them that way. Donna, I'd say, is a little prissy, if you know what I mean. She's very proper and spends a lot of time worrying about her clothes and her looks. I think she might be trying to grow up a little too fast. She doesn't play with the other dolls very much."

It was all true. Donna used to be a good friend, but she had grown too cool to hang out with Kat and Maggie even though she was only two years older.

"What's this doll's name?" Kat asked, holding up the one Twitch had first taken from the mantel.

Twitch paused. "Well, that's Kathryn, of course. I told you I modeled her after you."

"Kathryn!" Kat smiled. "What's she like?"

"Well, she's always been my favorite, you know. I kind of have a soft spot for her. She was so easygoing and friendly and she took such joy in everything. I noticed how she loved just walking in the snow in the early morning before anyone else was out and the whole world was unspoiled. And even as a tiny little thing she used to go out of her way to crunch the small piles of dried leaves in the fall. I could just see the revelry in her, the joy at such a simple, common sound. And what a competitor! She hated to lose at anything. If she was going to play, she wanted to win. She was a force among the other dolls too. Very popular, I'd say."

"Why do you say 'was'?" Kat asked, tears filling her eyes. "What happened to her?"

"She's just changed somehow," Twitch said, taking the doll from Kat and holding it close. "There is a sadness that has come over her and she's not herself anymore."

Kat quickly wiped the hot tears from her face.

"But it's okay. I know how she feels sometimes," Twitch said quietly. "I lost someone once who . . ."

There was a sudden bang in the basement and the tread of heavy feet up the stairs. Dr. Madison burst into the room. He was a big man, almost as tall as the door frame, with graying hair and small bespectacled eyes. "Well, well, Julia," he said to Twitch. "Our patient here seems to be doing much better."

"Oh, I do think that she'll be fine," Twitch said knowingly and backed away from the couch to make room for the doctor.

"Julia?" Kat said under her breath. "Julia. I can't believe it." She tried to sit up. "But, how. . .?"

"You're not getting up yet," Dr. Madison said. He took a pencil-thin flashlight out of his bag and shone it in each of her eyes. She had to follow his finger and answer some easy questions. He carefully felt each of her limbs and gently pressed on her stomach.

"You're one heck of a lucky lady," the doctor said to Kat and whistled. "What in the world were you doing up there on that ledge?"

Kat blushed and looked down at her hands.

"Well, come on, let's just get you home. Your father's beside himself worrying about you and he's got his hands full with Danny."

"Is Danny okay?" Kat asked.

"Yes. He's more scared than hurt. He woke up with a bad dream and decided to run home to his father. It was dark and someone left their Rollerblades out on the patio. He fell over them and hit his face up against the bottom step. He's just having a little trouble calming himself down. Come on, I'll help you up."

Dr. Madison pulled Kat to her feet and led her into the dining room to the basement door. Her back ached and her legs were stiff.

"The basement?" Kat said. "We're going in the basement?"

"Mrs. Twitchell never uses the front door. It's bolted shut. We'll go out through the basement—unless, of course, you'd like to try the window," he said slyly.

Kat blushed and turned to say good-bye to Twitch. "Thank you, Mrs. Twitchell. And I'm sorry for everything."

"Oh, you don't have to be sorry. But I do hope that you'll come back and visit me once in a while. And call me Julia."

"I will come back . . . Julia," Kat said slowly, searching in her mind for the memory of an old black-and-white photograph.

"Here," Twitch said. "Take this." And she handed Kat the doll that had her name.

"Oh no," Kat said, flustered. "I couldn't, really."

"Please take her. I want you to have her," Twitch insisted, pushing the doll into Kat's hands.

Kat thanked the old woman, tucked the doll under her arm, and descended into the basement. The steps had one of those glider chairs that worked like a ski lift to take you up and down.

"Need a ride?" Dr. Madison asked.

"No, thanks. I'm okay," Kat said, trying not to wince.

The room was lit by a single bare bulb hanging from the unfinished ceiling. The concrete floor was swept clean and spotless and the plaster walls were white and firm. Unlike her own basement where you had to jump over old tires and buckets and broken toys to get to the door, she and Dr. Madison breezed out in a few easy steps. Dr. Madison locked the door behind him.

The rain had stopped. The sky was still dark with swirling clouds, but they were thinning out and the light of the moon was hazily shining through to the street below. Dr. Madison walked Kat home and made her promise that she would stop by his office the very next day.

Chapter
28

THEY COULD HEAR DANNY quietly sobbing from his room when they got in the front door.

"I need to get going," Dr. Madison said to Kat. "Tell your dad that I'll talk to him tomorrow. And don't you forget to stop by the office so I can clean those cuts up a little better." Dr. Madison pulled on his cap and turned up the collar of his raincoat.

"Dr. Madison?"

"Yes, Kat?" He paused with his hand on the doorknob.

"Have you known Julia for a long time?"

"Yes, I have. Why do you ask?"

"Well, I thought that she . . . someone told me that she had jumped off the Tacony-Palmyra bridge."

Dr. Madison raised his eyebrows and released his grip on the door. "She did, Kat. A long time ago," he said quietly. "I was just a young boy, but I remember it well."

"And she survived?"

"She sure did. She was badly hurt but she made it. She was always something, Julia was." Dr. Madison shook his head and smiled.

"And she's always lived in that house?"

"Oh, no. She came back about fifteen years ago, after her husband died. Her parents had packed her off to live with some relatives out in Iowa until she got over her troubles. She ended up meeting a nice young man out there and getting married. They settled down in the Midwest."

"But her face . . ." Kat began.

"Julia was always a lot more than just a face, Kat. Besides, the damage to her face happened during a fire in Iowa. It's funny in a way; they say that she just couldn't bring herself to jump. By the time they got a ladder up to her she was on fire. I'll tell you what, though. That face bothers everyone else a lot more than it bothers her."

"She's got great eyes," Kat offered.

"So she does. But look, I've got office hours tomorrow and it's two o'clock in the morning. I have to go. You better get to bed yourself."

Dr. Madison left, but Kat stood, unmoving, in the middle of the silence of the house. She felt drained and powerless. It was as if all the circuits in her brain had overloaded and her mind had shut down. So she just stood and felt the quiet, and softly drew it around her like a blanket.

After a few minutes, she heard the door of Danny's bedroom click quietly closed. Her father came rushing down the stairs. He stopped just before her, dark circles under his eyes, his shirt wrinkled and stained.

"Oh, Kat," he said, pressing his hands to his forehead. Then he broke down, his shoulders collapsing and tears streaming down his face. He threw his arms around her and held her tightly. She didn't know why but she cried too— long, hard sobs that shook her whole body. Once she started she couldn't seem to stop. He held her wordlessly until she was too tired to cry anymore and then they both collapsed on the couch.

"I couldn't bear to lose you too," he said in a whisper, his eyes filling up again.

"Dad, I'm sorry I was so stupid. I don't know why I . . . ."

"It doesn't matter," he said, putting his arm around her. "I don't even care. As long as you're all right."

"Is Danny okay?"

"Well, he'll have a whopper of a bruise on his face tomorrow." Mr. O'Connor turned Kat's head toward the light. "Probably a lot like the one you're going to have."

"Oh, no," Kat groaned. "I wonder what Mom would think of us now. Do you think, when you're in heaven, that you can get embarrassed by your family on earth?"

"Are you kidding? She's probably up there right now passing your picture around to all the saints and bragging away."

Kat leaned back against his arm. "I miss her so much."

"I know. I do too. But we're going to be okay. We are."

"Promise me one thing," Kat said, turning to look in his face.

"What's that?"

"That you won't start having a new girlfriend every other month like Paul's dad."

"Oh, pleeeease," Mr. O'Connor sang, holding his hand over his heart. "I've got all I can handle right here."

Kat smiled.

He hugged her again. He pushed the hair back out of her face and kissed her forehead. "I think we should both probably get some rest now. Dr. Madison wants to see you tomorrow morning and you know Danny's going to be up at the crack of dawn."

They went up the stairs together and Kat fell exhausted into her bed.

Chapter
29

KAT SLEPT DEEPLY and without dreams well into the middle of the next morning. Her room faced east and the sun had risen above the rooftops of the houses across the alley and was now streaming in her window. It made a large rectangular splash of yellow above her bed. There was a soft knock at her door.

"Come in," Kat called.

Her father peeked in, then came and sat on the edge of her bed. "How're you feeling?"

"Okay, I guess," Kat smiled. She still had a slight headache and her back was sore but she didn't want to complain.

"I made some pancakes for you. Are you hungry?"

"You did? You mean the real kind?" In the last few months breakfast in the O'Connor house had consisted of dried cereal, packaged donuts, or microwave pancakes.

"Yep, the real kind. It wasn't that hard either. I just read what it said on the box and, well, I think they taste pretty good. Danny likes them." Mr. O'Connor brushed Kat's hair away from her face and examined the cuts and bruises on her left cheek.

"That's looking pretty nasty," he said, his voice full of concern.

"It's all right," Kat assured him, turning her head and sitting up. "IIow's Danny?"

"He's fine. Danny will always be fine. When I left him just now he was under the kitchen table supervising an enormous battle between the Indian nation and his dinosaurs."

Kat smiled at her father.

"The real question," Mr. O'Connor said, "is whether or not you and I will survive Danny's childhood."

They both laughed. "Can you imagine Danny as a teenager?" Kat asked.

"Oh, no," Mr. O'Connor groaned. "I don't even want to think about it. Why don't you get cleaned up and dressed? After breakfast you have to run over to see Dr. Madison. He already called once this morning to see how you were doing. And Maggie called about five times."

With her stomach full of thick pancakes and maple syrup, Kat set out for the doctor's office. It was almost noon and the weather was warm and delicious, golden and sweet like only an Indian summer day can be. How sad that Julia couldn't come out to enjoy this. Maybe she would pick some flowers from their windowbox and bring them to her this afternoon. Maybe she would sit and have some more of that lemon soother tea. Kat decided that she better make a quick stop at Maggie's and skipped up the steps to her front porch.

"Maggie?" she called through the screen door. "You there?"

"Kat! Come on in!" Maggie called. "I thought you would never come. Are you okay? What happened? What did she do to you? I was lying here all night with a crucifix on my chest. I felt so helpless. This stupid leg is driving me crazy. I couldn't get up to help you. Are you okay?"

"Maggie, calm down, I'm fine," Kat answered with a smile. "She's not a witch."

"What?"

"Twitch—I mean, Mrs. Twitchell is not a witch. You know who she is? You're not going to believe this. She's Sister Mildred's sister."

"No way!" Maggie stammered. "I don't believe it."

"It's true. And Maggie, she makes these great dolls."

"Kat! That's voodoo!"

"It is not. It's not like that."

"She's got you under a spell. Can't you see that? You're totally blind. What about her creepy house and all the things that she's done to us? Nice old ladies don't curse people."

"She never cursed us, Maggie."

"Then what's this," Maggie said frantically, pointing to her leg. "How'd this happen? And what keeps my dad from visiting me? And what about that watch that your mom gave you that just disappeared? What about all those things? They're not just coincidences, you know."

"Maggie, maybe they're just things that happen. I'm telling you, it doesn't have anything to do with Twitch. I thought you'd be glad. Anyway, I gotta go. I have to stop over Dr. Madison's office before he closes. But don't worry, I'll come back later on today and I'll tell you everything that happened."

"You're under a spell. You gotta believe me!" Maggie called after her as Kat went out the door and ran down the front steps.

Kat was Dr. Madison's last patient. He let her feed the tropical fish in the tank beside his desk and he cleaned her cuts and put an ointment on that made them burn. He taped some gauze on her face over the largest wound.

"I'm going to took like a geek," Kat said, trying to catch her reflection in the glass cabinet that held the medications and bandages.

Dr. Madison smiled. "Kat O'Connor, you will never look like a geek. Now get on out of here and stay away from second-story ledges."

Kat left the cool antiseptic office and stepped out into the sunshine. She didn't feel like going right to Maggie's. She stood on the corner for a few minutes, undecided, and let the sun warm her face and soak into her clothes. She walked aimlessly around the neighborhood for a while, until she found herself standing across from Patton Circle. It looked sad, like a deserted barracks after a failed war. The pigeons still hovered and pecked at the ground as though they clung to a forlorn hope that their friend and benefactor would soon return. He wouldn't. In the paper this morning it was reported that the General's lawyer would likely request a psychiatric evaluation. Her dad told her that the General would probably be placed in an institution where he would be taken care of. It made her feel better to think of him there than in a jail cell with murderers and drug dealers. She was the ranking soldier now. The only soldier. The General would want her to take over, to fill his shoes.

At the green light Kat went over to the circle and sat on the bench. Some of the birds waddled toward her, but she had nothing to offer them and they left. There was a cardboard box under the bench and Kat pulled it out. It was wet and crumbling. Inside were two smelly flannel shirts, a dirty worn jacket, and some leftovers from the food package she had brought the General only two nights ago. This was about all that was left of his life. His whole legacy.

She tilted her head back, resting it on the top rung of the bench, and closed her eyes. She imagined the General, feeding his birds, eating his rations, speaking with such deference to the transparent lady. He was ever a vigilant soldier, standing watch over his loss, preserving his pain, and zealously guarding his tragedy lest any of it slip away unawares with the passage of time. He stood his ground against the overwhelming power of time and refused to surrender his grief.

She wondered if he ever knew that Julia had come back or whether he was so attached to the transparent lady that he had lost all sight of the real one. And it had probably been Julia who had turned the General in, the man who had almost been her brother-in-law. She was always watching them play in the street and must have seen the whole accident unfold. Maybe she saw the license or recognized the old car. Maybe she remembered Michael, thrown from the jeep and killed, and felt the old pang at his loss. Turning him in was, Kat realized, the right thing to do. Julia was only protecting them all.

Someone touched her lightly on the shoulder. "Hey, Kat." It was Paul. "What happened? You okay?" he asked softly.

"Yeah, I'm fine," Kat said, quickly straightening up on the bench. She could feel the color rising in her face and she twisted her fingers in her lap.

Paul sat beside her and they silently watched the traffic motor around them for a few minutes. Paul cracked his knuckles.

"Look, I'm sorry about yesterday," Kat said, staring down at her shoes. "I know I kind of acted like a jerk, yelling at you and all."

"You didn't act like a jerk," Paul said.

Kat looked up at him.

"Well . . . maybe a little," he said and smiled.

Kat punched him in the arm. "And what about you?"

"Me? What did I do?"

"Abandoned me to Tyler Reid and his pack. That's what."

"You mean he did that to you?" Paul asked, his voice rising.

"No. No," Kat said, putting her hand over her bandaged cheek. "That's a long story. There's a lot I have to fill you in on."

Paul leaned forward on the bench with his elbows on his knees. "Look, Kat, I know you liked this General guy and all, and I don't want you to get mad again, but it really is pretty gross here. Can't we sit somewhere else?"

Kat looked around the weedy, trash-strewn island. She missed the General and she cared very much for him. But she couldn't take over his post. The warm beauty of this day, her feelings for Paul, and her love for her father and brother were all pulling her a different way. "Yeah, you're right," she said finally. "It is kind of gross here."

"Want to go do something?"

"Well," Kat said slowly, "I promised Maggie I would come over, but I was just thinking that maybe first I would stop by the gym and check out the Saturday basketball practice. They used to start around noon. Do you think it's too late for me to join the team?"

"For you?" Paul said with a quick smile. "No way. Can I walk you?"

"Sure," Kat answered.

And then out of nowhere he leaned forward and quickly kissed her. Kat felt her face flush, but she did nothing but stare at him, momentarily frozen by the surprise. Paul quickly looked away. As he sat back, a pigeon that was walking on the edge of the bench fluttered onto his shoulder. Paul bolted off the bench and shook his whole body. He was practically doing a dance, balancing on one foot and then the next, slapping at his clothes.

Kat burst into laughter. "Paul, it's gone! It was just a pigeon."

"Yeah, but those things are like rats with wings," he said, running his hands through his hair. "What if it gave me lice or something?"

Kat saw her chance. She took his hand and softly kissed him back. "I'm sure it didn't give you any lice."

"Can we please leave?" Paul begged.

Kat took one last look around the sad little traffic island. She felt a little guilty, like a deserter, but she knew that she wasn't going to come back. She performed a few final duties. She took the couple remaining pieces of bread from the food bag and threw them to the pigeons. She closed up the cardboard box and pushed it back in its place under the bench. She closed her eyes and thought of the General, barking orders, swaying to the silent music, grasping her hand as the invisible enemy marched forward and surrounded him. "I'm sorry, General," she whispered. "I'm sorry, but I've surrendered."

Kat took Paul's hand and they left Patton Circle behind. They walked up Cottman Avenue toward the gym, Paul still scratching at his head, checking for lice, and Kat's laughter rising up and mingling with the music of the city.